THE BIG HOUSE

THE BIG HOUSE

Naomi Mitchison

CANONGATE • KELPIES

First published 1950 by Faber and Faber Ltd.
First published in Kelpies 1987.

Copyright © 1950 Naomi Mitchison

Cover illustration by Alan Herriot

Printed in Great Britain
by Cox & Wyman Ltd, Reading, Berkshire

ISBN 0 86241 159 9

CANONGATE PUBLISHING LTD
17 JEFFREY STREET, EDINBURGH EH1 1DR

Mostly for
MURDOCH

CONTENTS

Chapter I

HALLOWE'EN

This was Hallowe'en, and the end of the black-out which had spoiled everything all these years. Half the children had been making false-faces and painting up their turnips for the lanterns, and a few of the grown-ups were out dressing, too. Port-na-Sgadan is kind of scattered, and before you had worked your way through from the shore to the glen, it would be late on, and you might have bumped yourself and stubbed your toes plenty stumbling about in the dark behind your false face. And you might get a rough welcome at one house or another, more especially if folks thought you were a lassie, and wanted to pull the false-face off you, but that was all in the game.

It was not in the game, though, for five or six big boys and girls, mostly in the qualifying class, to set on a school-fellow of their own, and knock her down and run away laughing as if it was the best joke in the world. She could, maybe, have dealt with two of them, as she was extra strong, the lassie, though she was little more than ten years old, but they were all at her. And some had sticks, and they broke her turnip lantern that she had been painting into a face all through the afternoon. So now she was on her hands and knees, under the lee of the byre wall, and her hand was bleeding, and there was muck on her face, and as soon as the others were out of hearing she began to cry hard and sore.

By and bye a boy came up to her, and she half stopped crying, only it had left her with a kind of hiccough in her chest, and the pain in her hands and arms, and her turnip smashed and Hallowe'en spoilt on her. The boy had no notion what to say, but he had heard from the others what had been done, and his evening was clean spoiled, too, for all he had his lantern and his false-face. He knew, and she knew, and each knew that the other knew, the reason why they had set on her. That was because she was from the Big House, and in times past the Big House ones had been hard and cruel to the fathers and grandfathers of the ones at the school, and kept them in fear and, maybe, put them out of their houses, but now the thing had turned round and they had revenged themselves. And it was all as senseless as could be, but there is the way things are. And the lad, whose name was Willie Macrae, but who was mostly called Winkie, stood there on one foot, and he was terrible affronted that this should have been done on Susan, but all the same there was no way he could get round to mention it. So all he said was "Hullo", and he gave a small kick at the broken bits of the turnip, and she said nothing, but only sniffed, and he could smell she was cut and bleeding, and yet it was beyond him to speak. He pushed his false-face round so that it was at the back of his head, with the beard he had made out of sheepskin wagging away behind his neck.

And then in a while they heard a piper a good way off, and it might have been one of the tinkers. But the nearer it came, the less it was like one of their own tinkers from the glen. And when it was quite near it stopped on the end of a bar. So they both looked at the corner of the barn, and Susan left off hiccoughing, and Winkie stood on both his feet, and the noise of a man walking fast came close, and the moon that was near full came half through a thinning in the clouds, and there was someone coming round the corner at them.

It is this way it always is at Hallowe'en. You can never be sure if someone you meet is themselves, and maybe out on their ordinary business, and not even remembering what night of the year it is, or if it is someone like yourself dressing and letting on that, whoever they are, theirself is the last person it is. It was the same for Susan and Winkie, and they could not be sure whether this was the piper or who it was, or whether it was a man or a woman even, for the face was in shadow, and the hair looked long and as though the wind had been blowing it, and the dress of the person was a kilt and a heavy plaid over it. And both of them knew that on Hallowe'en if it is a man dressing he will mostly be wearing woman's gear, and if it is a woman she will be wearing man's. So this could easily be a woman, and it seemed like it by the hair, and it was not terribly tall. But most of the men that had the kilts were none too keen on their wives wearing them, unless maybe it was an Army kilt, and Su thought quickly which of the men were back from the Argylls. But then they saw there was a beard on the person, but it was not sheepskin like Winkie's beard. And then they saw that the person had the pipes under his arm, and they knew by that it was not one of the Port-na-Sgadan women dressing for Hallowe'en, but a stranger and a good piper. And the moonlight shifted on him, and they were both frightened, suddenly and hard, and right down to their hearts.

Su was still on her hands and knees, but now she stood up, very quietly, touching the wall with her back and half holding to it. She was wearing her big brother's pyjamas, and a sword belt and scarf out of the dressing-up box, and

Norwegian ski stockings. Winkie was wearing an old red skirt of his mother's, and had trimmed his top half with a bit of something with balls and lace, which had once trimmed a mantelpiece. His father was a fisherman, and his two big sisters had gone out the other way dressed in their father's long woolly pants. The big girls mostly went off in a gang together, and would not have the wee ones with them.

Then the stranger said something, and at first neither of them understood, as it was not at all what they had expected, and he had a nice soft voice, and not a frightening voice at all. Then he repeated it, and Su giggled, for it was a phrase she knew in the Gaelic. Sometimes they had an odd bit of a Gaelic lesson at school when the schoolmaster was pleased with them, and when the piper asked in the Gaelic "where is the church", she knew the answer. Also, she knew that she pronounced it worse than anyone else in Port-na-Sgadan, and she whispered the answer to Winkie, who said it out loud. Then the man spoke again in the Gaelic, but longer this time, and neither of them understood properly. She whispered to Winkie to say to the man to come up to the Big House. She didn't want to go on any further now that her lantern was broken and her false-face was bashed. She wanted to go back to the house and switch on the electric light and make some cocoa, and not think about what had happened, and she whispered to Winkie to come back, too.

Winkie giggled, but he said the sentence. The piper shifted his pipes under his arm, and then he said gently, and still in the Gaelic, "I will not go to the Big House." And then he said, "Who are you?"

Su took a deep breath and said, "'*S mise nighean an Tigh Mhóir*." But she knew she was not sounding it right, just the same as she always knew she wasn't sounding her French right. But Latin didn't matter. The piper looked at her, and he smiled in the moonlight, and it was a surprise to Su to find that all her fright had gone away. This time he spoke in English, with the accent of the Highland people. "If indeed you are the daughter of the Big House, maiden, then you will be speaking the English, *ou bien le français.*" She answered quickly, *"Oui, je parle français."* But it wasn't really true, because she had only been learn-it a year with her mother in the holidays, and she was just showing off to Winkie, so she went on quick, "But let's talk English, please." She saw he was looking at her hard, and she suddenly wished she was in her proper clothes, so she said, "It's Hallowe'en."

"Och, yes," he said, "It is Hallowe'en again surely, and you are the guisers. But what is on your hand, maiden?"

"Oh," said Su, "I tumbled against a stone." And that was a show-off, too, but it made her feel much better. Then she said, "Come on."

He said, "It was the church I was looking for, but maybe the Big House will do."

"Come on, Winkie," said Su. "There's no one there but me." For she knew he felt kind of awkward coming to the Big House when any of the grown-ups were there. Even her mother, or her big brothers who were at school in England.

Well, then, they were just going round the corner of the byre when they heard folk coming. Both of them stopped, but the piper dodged into the dark of the byre-door behind them. Five people went by, grown-ups, all dressed and with false-faces and laughing. Susan and Winkie argued about who they were. Winkie was sure it was old Mrs. Macdonald from the smiddy's skirt on the man of the party, and the one with the navy trousers and its head in a flour-bag was Betty who worked at the Manse. Su said no, it was young Mrs. Paterson. "It was

Betty, right enough," said Winkie, "I knew her from the way she wiggled her behind."

"Well, then, if it was Betty," said Su, "the man would have been Red Tom, and he isn't that size."

"Betty hasna been going with Red Tom this month past," said Winkie, "she is after a slater from down the way."

"But——" said Susan, and then they both felt the hands of the piper on their shoulders, gripping them and holding them quiet. And this time it was hooves on the road, and someone went by the end of the byre on a white horse, and it was trotting hard. Whoever it was had a long cloak, and white boots with tassels on them, shiny in the moonlight, and a kind of small hat that was bright with tassels and bells. He went by, and the children looked at one another. By and bye Winkie whispered, "It must have been the horse from Baldonnacky, that is the only white horse there is."

"It was not," said Su. "This was a far bonnier horse, and not a working horse at all."

"And where else would it come from?" said Winkie.

"It was a real riding horse," said Su. "And, Winkie, did you see a kind of glitter on the bridle and along the reins?"

"Did you see it, too?" said Winkie, and she nodded. Winkie said, "I am dead sure, Su, yon was gold and diamonds."

The piper had taken his hands off their shoulders. "Let us go now," he said. And they could hear him breathing hard, like someone who has climbed a ladder over-quick.

"Come by the field," said Su, suddenly; she wasn't quite sure why. And round by the field they went, and along the dyke, and through the path in the rhodies. They had been moving quick to start with, but by the end they were all running, and Su let them in by the side door beyond the woodshed, and into the library. She switched on the lights, which weren't at their best, because the engine had been going wrong again, but still and all they were real electric lights, and always a great pleasure to Winkie. But the piper stared at them, and it came into Su's head that he had never seen such lights before. This was possible enough, though not usual, for most people had been by bus to some place where there are electric lights. She also noticed that the cut on her hand was a bit dirty, and Winkie said she had best put some iodine on it, so she went up to the bathroom, and while she was about it she thought she would take off the dressing-up clothes and forget what had passed. When she went to put on her frock, she thought no, she would put on her very best dancing frock, that was made out of a beautiful green silk dress of her mother's. And then it seemed worth while to wash properly, and even to brush her hair and put on her green ribbon. Then she took nuts and apples out of the dining-room cupboard, in case any of the guisers were to come in. There were only a few apples, rather withered, and cookers mostly, and the nuts wild hazel and half of them empty. All the time she kept thinking it was awfully silly to have asked this man in, and perhaps he was drunk or mad, but at least Winkie was there too, and it was sillier still to put on her best frock, and then at once afterwards no, it wasn't, and anyhow it was sucks on the ones who had knocked her down and meant to spoil Hallowe'en on her.

Well, down she went, and into the library, and there seemed to be no one there at all. But Su had played hide-and-seek so often that she got Winkie behind the log-basket almost at once, and said to him crossly, "What on earth are you doing, Winkie?"

He said, in a whisper, "There were steps going round the windows, and we hid."

"Where?" asked Su.

"In the big press," said Winkie, pointing to the chest by the piano.

"That's a daft place," said Su, "it's the first place they would look. Winkie, is it the police, or what?"

"No, it isna," said Winkie. "And he's no' a bad man. He—he is a good man, Su."

"Then, what's he frightened of? Who's after him, Winkie?"

Winkie came very close to her, and looked round and said, "It is Yon Ones, Su."

"The fairies?" said Su. "What rot, what utter rot, Winkie! I *won't* believe it!" And she stamped.

But Winkie looked really upset. "Watch out, Su," he said; "sure as you're there, it's true. He told me while you were up washing. And they might come in the house. What will we do?"

"But it just can't be true," said Su, "you know it can't! It just doesn't go with electric light! You're both trying to kid me on."

"Su," said Winkie. "What about the white horse with the gold bridle?" And then they heard horse hooves again.

"Get the Bible, Winkie, quick!" she said, and pointed. Then she picked up a couple of cushions and dumped them on top of the chest. Then the bowl of nuts and apples. Then the poker, which she stuffed under a cushion and sat on. Now Winkie had a grip of the family Bible, and brought it over and sat with her on the chest. She pushed an apple at him. Someone was coming in at the front door, that was never locked. Someone came across the hall, and they saw the door open.

It had been a frightfully quick swing between not believing and believing, and some way she had swung back already by the time the door opened, and she had her mind made up that it was going to be the policeman. But

16

it was nothing of the kind. It was a young man in a long green cloak, with the most beautiful wolfhound beside him. He stood there, looking at her, and he smiled, and before she knew what she was doing, she said, "*Fàilte ort!*" Then it was no use Winkie kicking her. The welcome was said, and the young man came into the room.

You know the way it is in late summer, when you are out by the sea after dark, and each step you take on the sand leaves a moment's glitter behind it? So it was with the young man's steps on the library carpet, and the dog's footmarks the very same. He was very fair, with bright blue-green eyes, and he had a gold collar on his neck, and gold bracelets, and the hound had a gold collar with square emeralds in it. Su felt awfully as though she wanted to get up and curtsey. He was so obviously a king or a prince. But her cold hand holding on to the iron of the poker anchored her to the top of the chest. The green-cloaked prince stopped smiling, and instead he frowned. As he did this his footprints, instead of sparkling light, were singeing and smoking. He bent his frown on Winkie and said, "Stand up." But Winkie had hold of the Bible, and Su shoved the poker at him, and Winkie remembered at the back of him how his own grandfather had needed to stand up and take his cap off to his betters. Winkie said, "No, I am a fisherman."

The prince stretched out his hand suddenly, and from each finger went flames. They kept shaping into twisted dragons and air fish and demons' horns, and they all jumped at Winkie and he yelped. "Stop it!" said Su. "Who are you, anyhow? You have no business here."

"Did you not bid me welcome, maiden of the green dress?" said the prince, and again he smiled.

"Not if you're horrid," said Su, and she felt she was being dreadfully rude, and supposing he was a king, and supposing she was doing the wrong thing. . . .

"I have gifts," he said, and he took a box out from under his cloak; it was a golden box, plain in shape, but with a wonderful pattern all over it of knotted flames and sea beasts. It looked as if it might be a jewel box, and Su suddenly made up her mind that he was going to offer her a magnificent diamond necklace, and she was equally certain that she was going to say no. But it wasn't. It was pre-war chocolates, the kind that Su and her brothers sometimes used to be given at Christmas by her London aunt who had been killed in the blitz in '41. You could tell by looking at them and smelling them that they were made with the very best chocolate, finely ground to melt like a dream on the tongue, and real butter and real almonds and walnuts and Brazil nuts and pistachio nuts, and real fruit and any amount of castor sugar, and not one bit of saccharine or soya flour or flavouring out of bottles. And you knew the soft ones would taste not of hair oil but of real cream and real juices and petals. And the hard ones would scrunch into grand mouthfuls, and beyond that there were marrons and crystallized fruit and apricots and tangerines, and those awfully good ones from the South of France, and glacé grapes that would crackle and pop in the mouth, and both Su and Winkie wanted them from the very bottom of their stomachs. There was always plenty to eat at Port-na-Sgadan, plenty of potatoes and oatmeal and herrings and milk, and a wild lot of turnips and cabbages, but there were no sweeties like this in all Europe, and never had been for Winkie, and never would be again for Su. For a moment it was pleasure enough only to smell them and eat them with their eyes. And then the prince held them out. Winkie looked at Su, and Su said, "I don't think we ought," but their mouths were filling with spit. Being hungry for sweets was a thing you didn't notice until they were there, but once it was on you it was terrible. And then the prince took a handful and poured them on to the chest between the two and the Bible and the withered cooking apples.

But even as he did it there was a noise in the hall, and under their eyes and stretching fingers the things turned to a scatter of leaves, and when they looked up there were five or six people coming into the room, all dressed and with their false-faces, and two of them baa-ing and letting on that they were sheep. Now in the ordinary way it can be frightening when the guisers come in at Hallowe'en, but now these were not frightening at all, but a pleasure, only what would they say to the shining fair prince? It then became apparent that he would be taken for a guiser, for he had wrapped his green cloak all over himself, and he was masked. Yet the terrible thing was that his mask was exactly the same as his face, only hard and brittle and with the smile transfixed on it. The beautiful hound was lying under the piano, in shadow.

Su whispered to Winkie, "Stay on the chest." But she herself had to get down and go over to her guests. They were big boys and girls, and suddenly she recognized Norah from the post office by the hair sticking out from the side of the false-face, and once you get one of the party, you will soon get them all, since you know who is likely to be going with who. Soon they were all guessed, and had their false-faces off, and were talking away together and eating the apples, and Norah whispered to Su, "Who is the man in the cloak?" Su said she had no idea at all, and Norah said it must be a Glasgow visitor, surely, and now the Hotel was open again you never knew who you mightn't see, and it could be a great film star, and he had a terrible good false-face.

Then two more peeped in through the door, kind of shy at coming in, but Su ran over, and by now she was beginning to wonder if there had been any truth at all in the things she had seen, the piper or the golden bridle or the box of chocolates. And she kept on thinking maybe the fair prince would have disappeared the next time she turned her head. She pulled one of the new lot in by the hand, and then she knew at once who it was, for she had been watching these same hands making a willow basket the day before on her way back from school. It was Ian Townsley, the young tinker, dressed in a woman's cotton dress that his mother must have begged off a farm years ago, by the fashion of it, and a false-face of stiff paper and willow twigs cleverly made. The other was his young sister, Dugaldina, in the queerest old pair of tartan trousers. Su guessed them at once, and brought them in and gave them apples, but they kept to themselves and hardly said a word, and the others didn't speak to them much. It was always the same way, and it was only Su herself and a few of the other children that would sit next the wee tinkers at school, or play with them, though they were extra clever at making things. It made Su wild and angry sometimes, for the wee tinkers were mostly a bit backward, because of them being on the road for one term of the year anyway, and the kind of looks and words they got were not helping them any to get over it. Even Winkie could be bad to them, and Su would pull his hair for him over it. So now she was dead keen to be nice to the two tinkers, and suddenly she said to Ian, "Do you have your chanter on you?"

Well, of course he had; he mostly always did. Whenever anyone asked him, and often enough when they didn't, he went into houses where they were playing the gramophone, to learn the tunes, and then he would be practising on the chanter. So Su asked him to give them a tune. He played much better when he was a bit drunk, but when the grown-ups were away the only whisky was in the flask upstairs, and that was for emergencies. Su didn't think this was one. In fact she was sometimes a bit worried in case she wouldn't know an emergency when she saw it.

Anyway, Ian Townsley struck up, and at first he was half shy, but everyone likes a tune, even if it is only the chanter and not the pipes, and some of them began to dance. Su was keeping an eye on the chest, but Winkie stayed sitting on it; he had his knife open in his hand, letting on he had been cutting an apple, but mostly because this was cold iron, handier to hang on to than the poker. But besides that, she was keeping an eye on the one in the green cloak; he was standing beside the curtains, and the light there wasn't too good because one of the top bulbs had gone, and nobody was likely to bother about it while the mistress was away. And Ian was trying one tune after another, some old and some new, and he was just on to a fresh one when the green-cloaked prince disappeared like a light switched off. Nobody noticed much, because he wasn't in the party, and he could easily have slipped out, but both the children saw, and both looked an one another. The wolfhound disappeared, too. Su crawled under the piano to make sure. She could smell its smell, and the floor was warm where it had been lying, but there was no dog. She thought it was the loveliest dog she had ever seen. And the loveliest chocolates. And the loveliest golden box. And the loveliest man. When she came up from behind the piano, she was very nearly crying. It was like the time she had got measles just before Peter Pan.

So after a bit they all said good night. They must be going, and it had passed the evening fine, and they picked up their false-faces and coats and sticks and turnips and went off. The tinkers went off together behind them. Dugaldina had hardly said a word all evening, she was that shy, and nobody had danced her but Su.

When they were all gone Su said to Winkie, "What happened?"

Winkie said, "He has gone, anyhow, him and his sweeties."

"But did we dream him all, or what?"

"No fears, he was there right enough."

"But how could he have been?"

"By jings, he was," said Winkie. "Will we open the press now?"

"I bet it will be empty," said Su. "But you can if you like."

They moved off the things and opened the lid, and Su was dead sure there wouldn't be a thing in it. But there was. The piper was there with his plaid right over him, and Su said, "It's true, after all."

The piper sat up. "You did well, the two of you," he said, "and That One is away and will not be back yet awhile." He put a leg over the side of the chest; he had knitted stockings and odd shoes of rough leather laced together round the edges. His kilt and plaid were lovely: the woollen stuff and the dyes soft on the eye and hand with wear and weather. His hair was a bit long, and he had a short dark beard. The plaid was pinned on his shoulder with a brooch that somehow had the same look as the golden box. He sat down on the lid of the chest, his pipes behind him. The drones were ivory, and the mounts looked to be gold. He was not very big, which was just as well, or he would have been squashed in the chest. He looked round. "How at all were you guarding me? Aye, cold iron and the Book." He held out his hand, and Su gave him the Bible. "It's long enough since I have seen a Book. Will we try it now?" He handed it to Su, who shut her eyes, opened it and pointed. Then she read it out:

"And thou shalt not escape out of his hand, but shalt surely be taken, and delivered into his hand; and thine eyes shall behold the eyes of the king of Babylon, and he shall

speak with thee mouth to mouth, and thou shalt go to Babylon."

Su looked round at Winkie, hoping he was not going to take it seriously, but he was white, and his mouth half open, and the piper looked rather grave. "That is not so good," he said.

"But it's all rot," Su said, "and it doesn't work like that." And she stamped, and suddenly she was tired and her hand was smarting and she wanted to cry, and she did cry.

"Let me have a try," said Winkie, and opened the page and pointed. "That's better!"

"Blessed be the Lord my strength, which teacheth my hands to war, and my fingers to fight:

"My goodness, and my fortress; my high tower, and my deliverer; my shield, and he in whom I trust; who subdueth my people under me."

"Oh, you cheat," said Su. "I could see you looking for a good one."

"I was not," said Winkie. "If I had been I would have had the one about bashing yon dragons."

"Now you", he said to the piper. Again they waited, and this time the piper read out:

"And when she had opened it, she saw the child: and, behold, the babe wept. And she had compassion on him."

"It is beyond me to know what is meant by this, but it will be shown. Aye, aye, doubtless it will be shown."

"Well, I don't believe in it," said Su. "It might have been a list of the Kings of Israel, or one of the bits that say *Selah, Selah,* like in Religious Instruction."

"It might have been," said the piper. "But it was not."

Chapter II

THE HELPERS

———————————————

Su, sniffing suddenly, minded on the fact that she was hostess, and she should get the piper something to eat. "Anything at all," he said, "anything at all. But maybe I should bide a while in case your servants should make their observations?"

"Servants!" said Su contemptuously. "There's only old Morag, and she will be reading the *People's Friend* in bed."

"One servant only—here at the Tigh Mór?" said the piper.

"Here at the Tigh Mór," said Su. "Don't you know there's a war on?" Winkie giggled. "Well, a peace anyway, and there won't be anyone else until Mother comes back from her horrible Ministry, except when the boys are home from school, so that's that. And anyhow, servants are a nuisance. Not letting you cook."

"Well, well," said the piper, "times have changed plenty."

"Since when?" asked Su suspiciously.

The piper leaned forward. "Would you try now to believe me a wee small bit?" Su nodded. "I have been with the Fair People for twice seventy years, and it is a prince of their people who is seeking me."

The Helpers

"You mean—in the fairy hill? But it *can't* be! It doesn't make sense."

"What else makes sense with what you have seen with your own eyes?"

She stood a long time, frowning, and nothing came any clearer. At last she said, "Do *you* believe it, Winkie?"

"Aye," he said, "he told me while you were up cleaning yourself. I had no difficulty at all in believing him. It is just the way these things have not happened so much lately, or maybe they are kept out of the papers. Yon one with the box: I knew in my mind he was a prince sure."

She nodded, and went to the door. Mostly she didn't mind being alone in the house or anything, but now everything had gone queer, and it seemed a long way between the library and the kitchen. She just had to dodge back from the dark and catch hold of Winkie and say, "Do come along to the kitchen! Let's all come."

Well, it was one of those big old kitchens, with a big range and brass and steel work, and pots and pans from the time folk thought nothing of eating half a sheep. But the range was cold, and the pans long cold and clean, and in one corner there was a nice wee Esse stove, warm and purring a little. Su lifted up the lid and put on a small pan of milk. Winkie knew where the cocoa lived. It was a bad time of year for eggs, but there was a paper of herrings that Winkie's father had given her. Su hated gutting herrings, but Winkie hopped out his knife and gutted them and took out the big bones, and then they dipped them in oatmeal and threw them into the frying pan. "I don't suppose you got any herrings in the fairy hill, Mr. —— What is your name?" asked Su, at which he smiled.

"My name is Ferguson, but my first name is Donald, and they called me Donul Beg because the others in the family were big men. Aye, aye, and it is big coffins they will be lying in now."

It was bread-and-marge scrape, because, as usual, the butter ration was finished. And if he stays he won't have a ration card, Su thought in a worry. She put saccharins in the cocoa. But the herrings were as good as only fresh herrings can be.

"Aye," said the piper as he took his second. "So this is mortal food. When I was a wee fellow it was mostly herrings we had, and salt herrings all winter. I mind well on the taste and smell of them. But we had not the white bread. It is a queer kind of butter you have."

"It isn't butter," said Su. "It's Friday. It's always marge by then."

He shook his head and ate. Winkie whispered to Su, "We'd better explain to him."

"O.K. You do."

"Nae fears. You do."

They made faces at one another rapidly. Then at last Su said, "We've just had a war."

"Aye, aye," said the piper. "It was always so."

"But this was bigger. It was everywhere almost."

"There was a terrible great war in my own time," said the piper, "against yon Napoleon."

"We had Hitler, who was much worse," said Su, "but he's been bumped off. And—no, you tell us about yourself first." She stuck her elbows on the table and leant forward. "Can you stay, Winkie? They'll not be missing you?"

"Och no, not at Hallowe'en," he said, and began to unwind the stuff from round his top half.

The piper said, "Well, it is all simple enough. I was over on the far side with my pipes, playing at a wedding, and coming back with the drink in me. Then, at Knocnashee, the Fair People stopped me on my road, and asked me to come in and play for them, and I, being a wee bit past my right senses with the drink, went in and played."

"What language did they speak?" asked Su.

"The Gaelic, surely, the same as myself."

"But you speak English now."

"Ach, they gave me the gift of tongues. I could speak to you in your own tongue if you were a black heathen. They gave me other gifts. But the time came when I wanted back to mortal earth. And it had seemed a matter of days there in the Hill, but it was seven years already. Now I got word to my wife that she could win me if she would at Hallowe'en, but the Fair People would change my shape on me, and she must hold me fast. So at Hallowe'en I came back to my own house, and sat down at my own table, and the cradle bairn was a big boy, and my wife was older. Yet she did as I bid and threw her arms round me. But they changed me into foul and frightsome shapes. And at last she was so frighted she let go of me, and I was back in the Hill and the chance gone."

"Oh dear," said Su. "Oh, I am sorry!"

"It is long ago, lassie, but it was bitter enough at the time. Yet they gave me gifts again. And whiles I piped to their dancing, and whiles it was myself that danced. And as we swung in the dancing we would see shapes beautiful beyond all kenning, and they became real to us, and we lived year upon year with these shapes and appearances. And the next time for the door to open it was seventy years on. But I would not go. I was feared of what I would find. If there were any of my folk left, they would be old beyond knowledge. My bairn would be an old ancient man, with death waiting for him. It was beyond me to face the thing. But to-day is twice the seventy, and all will be clean again, or will be forgot and swept into the past. So I have come back. But they cannot bear that anyone should go from them, so the prince is hunting me."

"Why at all did you play the pipes coming down into Port-na-Sgadan? Surely they must have heard you?"

"They could follow me, anyway, when they chose. And I needed to give myself courage coming back into a time so far beyond my own."

"But how are you going to be saved this time?" said Su.

"I was thinking that if I got to the church I might be safe. Yet I was not certain. But now it is borne in upon me that the thing will be done by a maiden, and that will be yourself."

"Golly," said Su. And then, "Well, I might try, but I don't know. I say, why did the Prince disappear?"

"It was the tune. That tune was well known in my time. It is the same as cold iron or rowan berries or the Book itself. Yon lad that played it will not know that there is anything to it, and it is laid on me that it is the one tune I must not play, but I will teach it to you." He looked at Winkie.

"I canna play the pipes," said Winkie, alarmed.

"I've seen you try," said Su hopefully.

"Aye, but not well enough for this."

"Ian Townsley would be more use than you," said Su.

"Ach, Ian's only a tink!"

"He's away better than a fisherman, anyway!"

"You wee devil, Su. If you werena a lassie I'd sort you!" And then he saw the bump on her forehead, and the cut on her hand, red and yellow with bruising and iodine, and suddenly a thing shifted in his mind, and he said, "Well, if it was yon last tune, I'll maybe make shift to whistle it." He was a good whistler, the best whistler in the school, but often enough getting into rows for it, the way he would whistle during sums without knowing he was at it at all. He tried the tune over, but the first time it was not just right, because it rose suddenly a whole octave, the way the pibroch does, and he had got the wrong interval. But the second time he tried it over—"Oh, you're hurting me!" Su squealed and jumped up from the table.

He stopped, and the piper came to her quick, saying, "What is it, my darling?"

"I don't know!" Su said, with her hands up to her mouth, "but it hurt all down my back, like a knife!"

"Wait, you," said the piper, and got up. "Now, stand near yon light, but a bit to the side. Aye, so. Ach, isn't that hellish altogether! He has stolen your shadow on you, my poor wee lassie, and taken it away."

"Oh no!" said Su, trembling a bit. The piper put his arms round her; she could smell the kind of heathery, peaty, comforting smell of his beard and plaid.

"You shall have it back, *mo chridhe*, even if I need to go back myself in your stead. I am feared this came about with yourself wearing the green dress and saying the word of welcome. But indeed it is late on in the year, and folks willna be noticing at all. So you needna fash yourself any on that score. It is mostly in summer that it is so clear and so affronting when this has been done on folk. But we will need to see what can be done. Is there not any kind of a helper here that we could count upon?"

"A helper? There's the Home Guard," said Su doubtfully.

Winkie, watching, said, "He doesna mean that, Su. He means—ach, well, he just means the Brounie."

"But it's all rot, really!" said Su.

"Are you that sure, Su?" Winkie asked. "There's folks at Port-na-Sgadan that wouldna agree with you."

"Oh," said Su, "nobody in the house has seen it for a hundred years."

"Aye, because you Big House ones didna need it. But who put in the coals for my own mother's brother that

was living in the shore cottage yon night of the big gale?
And who covered your own gardener's seedlings in the
May frost three years back?"

"Well, I never heard about it," said Su.

"There is things that dinna get told to the Big House
ones." said Winkie. "Ach, dinna look at me yon way, Su!
You arena telling me everything out of your own doings!
But maybe we might ask the Brounie to give us a bit
hand."

"But I don't know how to ask it!"

"It could be," said the piper, "that your guardian has
been by us the whole time."

Su and Winkie looked at one another. Then, very carefully, both of them looked round. Sure enough, the
Brounie was sitting on the dresser, among the big old
ashets that were never used nowadays. The Brounie had
a nice face. If you think of the kind of face a robin would
have if it were a person, then that was the sort of face the
Brounie had. If you think of the size of the size of a sheltie as com-
pared with a riding horse, then that was the size of the
Brounie to a man's size. He had clothes the colour of
winter leaves, or mahogany furniture, and dark bright
eyes. Su looked away quick, and then looked again. The
Brounie was still there. The Brounie said to the piper,
"Gie's a reel!"

The piper said, "We are in danger."

"Ach, what's about it!" said the Brounie. "Danger can
wait, dancing canna. But gin you're feart, I'll set the seal
on the doors." It pointed its finger. Out hopped the keys
from the dresser, and over to the two doors and locked
them, and the shutter and bar came up over the window
the same as if it had been black-out. "Cauld iron," said
the Brounie and grinned. "Fill your bag, *mo bhalach*!"

"It'll wake Morag!" said Su.

"It will not," said Brounie. "She is sleepin fu' sound

and in a sweet remembrance of her past sins. They werena muckle, puir betch!" it added. The piper was blowing on his bag now, and reaching up a hand to tune the drones to his liking. The Brounie had hopped down, and was speaking to him in the Gaelic, and he nodded, smiling with his eyes the way his mouth was busy at the pipes. Su and Winkie had pushed back the kitchen table, and sat on the top of it. The piper broke into a march, walking up and down quick across the width of the old range. Then he stopped and went into a reel and strathspey. They were tunes which neither of the two children knew. Oh, there was dancing! The Brounie might be wee, but he was nimble as a bunch of sandhoppers. He leapt high, snapping his fingers, doing the grand double and treble cuts. The piping shook and bounced through the kitchen, yet it seemed unlikely that it could get past the iron. Winkie and Su sat, swinging their jigging feet, their fingers tapping on the table. The dancing pulled the low cries of encouragement out of the backs of their throats. The Brounie held out his hands, and they slipped off the table, and were into a reel of three with him. They were doing steps that they did not know were in them to do. The soles of their feet were like steel springs under them, and though the Brounie was shorter a bit than themselves, yet when he held hands with either of them for the swing, whether it would be behind or before, with one arm linked or the other, they span in the twist like autumn leaves, like the dry keys spinning from the ash tree. Winkie had kicked off the old skirt and his boots forby, and was dancing barefoot in his shirt sleeves. Su had a wee thought of pleasure at her bonny silken dress that was only right for such dancing. But at last the tune that had been mounting and mounting seemed to spring clear of the pipes altogether, and the sudden silence came on them like a dive into cool water. The piper and the Brounie were speaking to one another in the Gaelic too quick for the two to follow. Su poured out the rest of the cocoa for the Brounie and got some oatcakes out of the tin.

"He says", said the piper, "that you will be in no shape to save me, but rather in danger for yourself, until you get back your mortal shadow, and you will not get that until you go into the Hill for it. And there, my poor lassie, is the meaning of your text."

"Have I *got* to go?" said Su.

"You will need to decide that for yourself," said the piper.

"Well, I won't," she said.

There was a small silence. Then Winkie said, "Could I not go for her? She is only a lassie."

"No, I'm going myself!" she said. "I—I only wanted to see what you'd say." That wasn't true, but they all let on that they thought it was. "Only how do I get into the Hill?"

"Ye'll no' get the day," said the Brounie, "the way yon Ministry of Supply felled the trees any which way at all, and a wild bing o' roots and stones ower it. The daft clowns, cuttin' on Knocnashee, and they could ha' jaloused there was a bit thing wrong, the way their axes were blunting on them!"

"Well, then, how *do* I get?"

"Ye'll need to gae back a whilie."

"Into the past?" she said. And at once she remembered all E. Nesbit's books, which, of course, she had read, and the whole thing suddenly became more feasible. "But *when* in the past?"

"Ach, any time at all," said the Brounie, and began singing to himself, to a strathspey tune, "Ony time, ony time, ony time ava——"

"Let them go back to my own time," said the piper, "and maybe I will be able to keep an eye on them."

The Helpers

"Aye, but you willna ken whatna bairns they are."

"I kind of half might," said the piper.

"Will I go, too?" asked Winkie eagerly.

"Aye, aye," said the piper, "you had best go with your lassie, and mind you of your text."

"But how long will it take?"

"Ach, there's no telling at all. It could be days or weeks, or months even."

"But they'll be missing me at home!" said Winkie. "How can I gang?"

"It's all right, Winkie," said Su, remembering *The Amulet* and *Harding's Luck*. "It doesn't take any of time now. That is right, isn't it?" She appealed to the piper, who nodded. "What will we do when we get to the Hill?"

"You will not take their gifts and, above all, you will not eat," said the piper.

"I do hope they won't try and give us sweeties like last time," said Su, and sighed.

"You will need to be strong and steadfast, my lassie, as befits one from the Tigh Mór, because if you are not that you can neither lead nor help nor think for your folks, and then you are nothing. You are less than a wee beetle on the floor." And he put his foot on one of the nasty little scuttling silver fish that were for ever going in and out under the old range, and then he said to Winkie, "If you see a way for her, your hands will be strong to fight." He bent down to his stocking-top and took out the *sgian dubh* from there. It was a most beautiful knife, hilted with bog oak, and a good grip on it, and in the top an amethyst-hearted thistle. "Take you this, laddie. Maybe it will serve you. It is fairy iron and no' the cold iron of mortal earth. Mind, now, if you stab to kill, go up under the ribs and behind the fold of the plaid."

Winkie put his hand on it, and there was a great blush

33

of pleasure sweeping from one side of his face to the other.

"Oh, you are lucky!" said Su. "You might really be able to kill someone!"

"You will go back holding hands," said the piper, "and holding hands, you will come back to now."

"Is that all?" said Su.

"Ye'll maybe find it none sae easy tae hold a hand o' his in yon days, my dawtie!" said the Brounie, and chuckled.

"But won't we have to say a spell or something?"

"Your shadow will whisper to you."

"But will my shadow be there? I mean—will it be *then*?"

"Ach, yes," said the piper, "in the Hill, time is away different. But whereabouts it will be, that is beyond me. Yet I can tell you one thing. It is no use at all looking for the mouth of the Hill; it will come on you sudden. And you must not tamper with time past to make it come. Let the times gang their own gait, and yourselves fall in with them, and sooner or later the mouth of the Hill will be there, and the two of you together at the threshold. But unless you are together you will not go in."

"But what will the other people think of us? Will they —I mean, will we be somebody who is there anyway? And will we know what to do and all that?"

"Dinna fash yoursels for that," said the Brounie, "I will be there, and I'll gie ye a bit shove if the thing doesna gae just right."

The piper added, "Your bodies will be of that time, but your minds will be of now."

"Oh," said Su, worried, "will my then body have its shadow?"

"Aye, aye," said the piper, "but now you should go, and we will be waiting for you in this very place. Hold hands, now, the two of you."

The Helpers

"But how long will you wait?"

"See yon wag-at-the-wa'?" said the Brounie, pointing to the kitchen clock. "When it gaes left ye'll gang, when it gaes right ye'll be back. Watch now!"

The pendulum of the clock wagged to the left.

Chapter III

WHAT HAPPENED TO SU

Su opened her eyes again, and a pair of brown eyes looked back into hers. Like Winkie's. But not Winkie. But someone she knew as well as she knew Winkie, if once she could get the thing disentangled. Someone was wearing a long dress of brown-and-white checked linen, and a muslin apron and a collar with long ends; her hair was in long ringlets under a white ribbon. She put her finger to her lips, "Wheesht now, Su!" They were hiding in behind the cane settee in the drawing-room. Yes, that was it. The fireplace just the same, and the fire-irons, and some of the furniture, but different pictures and the most lovely curtains, embroidered with birds and great flowering trees. They had been playing hidey with their cousins, she and Elspeth. Yes, it was all coming untwisted inside her, and when it was their turn to run she was quite used to running in a long dress and silly little slippers, and of course she knew her cousin Jockie that caught her. It was as though the right words came into her mouth to say, and she only noticed after a while that she herself, the same as all the rest of them, was speaking with a broad accent and using more Scots words than she ever thought she knew, but now they ran off her tongue.

36

What happened to Su

When the grown-ups came in the children all scuttled out of the drawing-room and played all over the house. It was raining outside, but there were big fires in all the rooms, and the smell of peats drifting through the place. At first when she saw the grown-ups it was a surprise to see the men dressed in knee breeches and coats, mostly in dark cloth, but at least not black, and two of the younger ones in tartan trews, and all with lovely lace and linen ruffles, and her grandfather wearing a wig. And the ladies were in long silk dresses, cut low, the younger ones with bare arms, and gold bracelets sliding on them; they had beautiful Indian shawls or scarves slipping off their arms and shoulders, and Granny and Aunt Jean had lacy caps. But why, after all, be surprised? How else do grown-ups dress?

So now for days and days Su had the loveliest time with her cousins, living in the house with them, and all the fun and people and life going on. It was the same house, but changed, and made alive and lit up with voices and candles, music and mealtimes. It was as different as could be from living there by herself with nobody but old Morag, and the boys away, and never going to London because of the war and the house being blitzed, and the others at Port-na-Sgadan school who wouldn't really make friends, nor play the same pretend games, nor read the same books as herself, and hardly ever asked her to their houses, not even Winkie. And the awful feeling of being different. Being alone. Now this was like—oh, it was like before the war again. Su was happy the way she had forgotten how it was to be happy.

There was her special friend Elspeth, and Elspeth's big sister Euphemia, and her wee sister Mysie, and Isabel and Helen forby. They had a kind of play-house, like a sort of huge doll's-house room, about eight feet square, with furniture and cups and plates, and knives and forks, all

37

wee, and they played immensely long and complicated make-up games here with their dolls and the two younger boys. They decorated the table for wedding parties and christenings, with all the wee-est flowers and mosses, and got real food for the dolls to eat. It was like the deepest kind of inside, the play-house. You felt safe and close and snug as winter mice, and the trembling shivering blobs on the mosses were like tiny emeralds, and the tiny faces of heather and eyebright and wild pansy, seen close, were as important as people. In her other life Su didn't play with dolls, and was inclined to turn up her nose at the little girls who did, but here it was just part of the way they were all living, and a fascinating and delightful thing to do.

But there were other games. There were skipping games with rhymes to them. There were singing games. There was French and English, and of course there were lessons, but no school! No shoving and bullying and getting into gangs or having a gang against you. No horrible lavatories and scruffy playgrounds and rubbed paint and nasty, smelly old desks. They learnt to play the spinet and harp. Su had always wanted to play a great gold harp, and only wished there had been a glassy sea, too. They learned needlework and the making of various exciting kinds of jams and preserves and ointments; they learnt to make syllabubs, milking into china bowls full of white wine and sugar, until the whole thing was a delicious sweet froth. The china bowls were Lowestoft, whole sets of them painted with small bright wreaths and bows, with the coat of arms that she knew well enough. It occurred to her at first that there was one of these bowls carefully put away in the glass-fronted cupboard at home in the other life. But after a bit that went clean out of her mind, along with plenty else.

Most days there would be dancing sooner or later, more especially if there were visitors, and the children wild to

be at it and hiding, the way they would not be sent to bed
before the fiddlers started in, and after that there would
surely be one of the grown-ups to beg them off for a
dance or two, and it would be a queer thing if they were
not there for half the evening at least, and getting their
share of the oranges that were passed round. Mostly they
were in sets by themselves, or if one of the servant lassies
came in she would be caught up with them, or maybe one
of the ghillies come in to the house with a message or
waiting to take a letter. In some dances, such as the Cir-
cassian Circle or the Roundabout Hullachan, the whole
company would dance with one another, and once in a
while one of the children would be snatched off to make
up a set with their elders. It would mostly be to the
fiddles, yet there would be times when the younger men
would all take it into their heads to be wearing kilts and
doublets, and then they would be sure to have a piper or
more likely two.

Su, thinking back on it afterwards, had wondered at
first to see so few kilts either on the men of the Tigh Mór
or the men about Port-na-Sgadan. But when she hunted
about for a reason she saw it was because the family were
Whigs, followers of the Duke. For more than fifty years
they had looked on the kilt as a symbol of the beaten and
despised Tories, and were only now beginning to wear it
as a show-off and because the old enemy was forgotten.

Certainly they looked well enough in it, and the ladies
in high-waisted white satin and tartan scarves. At one of
these dances Su, to her pride and delight, was picked by
one of her cousins for a set with the glittering grown-ups,
dancing with her bare arms lifted in the midst of a swirl
of tartan and lace. They cried encouragement to her as
she leapt like a thin light flame, and afterwards she heard
her partner speak of her: "You'd say the Brounie himself
had taught the lassie!" And at that a thing came darting

through her, and she looked at the piper and, sure enough, it was their own piper. He nodded to her and smiled, but the men were all round him and he might have done that anyway for a young lassie of the house, and before she could get speaking to him she and Elspie and the rest had been swept off to bed.

There were any amount of folk doing one thing and another in and around the house, and all gathering in to meals in the big servants' hall beyond the kitchen. There were grooms and dog boys, and the head coachman with his great wig, and the housekeeper who wore black cloth on weekdays, and black silk in hundreds of gathers under an embroidered apron on Sundays. And there were all the lassies who scrubbed the floors and carried the pails up and down, and turned the meat and washed the dishes and mended the children's clothes. They talked the Gaelic among themselves, and mostly all of them went barefoot, having only the one pair of shoes, which they wore on Sundays and at family worship.

Morning and evening there were always prayers, and some days they would be long and dreich, and everyone fidgeting, but other days they would be short and a nice cheery psalm to one of the good tunes. The servants all came in and sat on benches, which they brought with them, with the housekeeper and the head coachman leading them, like a string of ducks. And on the Sabbath Day they all went to church in a row, and the family sat in the front pew with the servants in behind them. The services seemed to go on and on, and the sermons droning away all in one voice, but if you did not listen and keep quiet you might be breaking the Sabbath, and there of a sudden was hell opening in the very floor of the pew!

And yet it was also at these times, when the life of the body was stilled, that Su's mind woke up again. She suddenly became her old self, looking out with her own eyes, and comparing things and turning over what she had seen and heard and smelt and tasted and done. That way she would think suddenly that it was awful silly to have all these maids hanging around in the house and not even proper mops and brooms for them, let alone a Hoover! And taking water from the spring and carrying it up-stairs all the time instead of having baths. Not even a kitchen sink, and all the water needing to be heated by the fire, so that there was never really enough hot water. But still people never thought of having baths more than once a week, and often enough not even that, so the whole lot of them were—yes, they were niffy. One didn't notice it unless one thought, and all the grown-ups—the ladies and the men, too—using an awful lot of scent. And talking of bathrooms——! Golly, they are a dirty lot. *We* are, I suppose. And all the servants having to do it, carrying everything downstairs. Only they don't seem to mind. *Why* don't they mind?

And then she would think worriedly about Winkie, and try to peep round for him, and most likely get a sharp pinch from whoever was sitting next her. And she never could get a sight of him. Even when they and the rest of the heritors were walking in late and proud through the body of the kirk. And there was no sign at all of the fairy hill. And when the sermon was going on and on she would turn over in her mind all that she had heard the grown-ups talking about but hadn't maybe heeded at the time. And she would make up her mind to listen well next time instead of whispering with her cousins and playing the kind of secret games one plays under one's breath almost in a roomful of grown-ups, and that some-times sets one off into uncontrollable and unexplainable giggles.

Yet when it came to the bit she never could listen much, any more than any of the others did. The grown-ups' things were dull, and the children had a world of their own which only sometimes intersected with the grown-ups' world. At mealtimes they sat all in a bunch at one end of the table, needing to mind their manners and not speak except they were spoken to. The food was good enough, and any amount of it, but gey badly cooked, for all the kitchenmaids and scullery boys. Still and all, if you left anything on your plate, there were plenty dogs to give it to, and nobody minding. There were no vegetables, but that was no hardship to Su who was always being made to eat horrible greens in the other time. They drank beer or goats' milk, which was thought to be strengthening, and often they would go down to the dairy for butter-milk and cream. Almost all the things they had for des-sert were made with cream, and sometimes they were each given a glass of sweet wine. Again, after the first wee surprise, Su took it all as a matter of course.

When they did happen to listen to the grown-ups talk-ing, it seemed to be all about other families and an awful lot about the Duke, or else it was about politics and the wicked French, who had cut off the King's head and had set up instead an Emperor who was called Napoleon, and he was the same as one of the awful things in Revelations. Or else they would speak about the English and doings in London. At first when she heard the word London, Su used to feel a wee kind of jolt, and her mind would start up, but the Su whose body she wore had no interest in London, had never been to the Zoo, or Kensington Gar-dens, or up and down in the lift at Harrods. But the whole of the other life was becoming dimmed anyway, and after a matter of weeks the old days of rationing and black-out and then the end of the war which hadn't meant much yet, and the lonely empty house and the broken asphalt playground and flaring Tilley lamps of the school, were almost as far away as pre-war London.

What happened to Su

But at night with the sleepy body losing grip of things, the mind woke up again in Su. They slept in a long low room, two to a bed, and sometimes they would be planning and whispering and giggling until they fell asleep in the middle of it, and that was fine. But if they didn't, Su would worry and fall on sleep fashing and hashing over what was to do, since there had been no sign of the fairy hill and no sign of Winkie. Then, too, she would think of what she minded of the grown-ups saying at table. When they spoke of the politics they were always angry at Jacobins and such, and the common people getting uppish and speaking against their betters, and wanting more of one thing or another, and maybe burning ricks, or getting together to ask for more wages, against all law and decency. That would mostly be in other parts of Scotland, and most of all round Paisley and Kilmarnock, away among the weavers and bonnet-makers and such, but it might spread. They talked about it as if it were the measles, Su thought, and not—not people.

And then one day the uncle she liked least of the grown ups, because of his way of tweaking her nose or pulling her hair for fun, began telling them how he had caught Dougal, the tailor's young brother, cutting a tree —stealing the tree by cutting it—and had the fellow well thrashed and sent off to the recruiting sergeant, thus giving a needed recruit to the Army, and giving a lesson to the neighbourhood on the sin of theft. The rest had all laughed, and said that was the right thing to do surely, it would teach them; they were a sullen rebellious family, and this tailor fellow a centre of disaffection, and he used the money he made sewing breeches to buy papers from the terrible agitators in Glasgow. And it was queer how most of the fishermen had enough English to understand such things, though they could not understand a clear order from their betters! You needed to have a tailor

43

about the place, but a man with a trade was the first to become contumacious and a spreader of anarchy and Jacobinism. "They are needing a dose o' Lord Braxfield's medicine," said one of the men, and everyone laughed. Su didn't know what that meant, but it had a cruel sound to it somehow.

That night she turned over and poked Elspeth. "Elspie, what ava will happen to yon man that has been made into a sodger?"

"What, Dougal?" said Elspeth sleepily. "Ach, he was a wicked man and he will gang awa to fecht the wicked murthering Frenchies."

"But what way was he wicked, Elspie?"

"He was a thief. He brak the Eighth Commandment."

"Aye, but maybe he was needin' the wood. It was nocht but an auld deid tree, Elspie."

"But it wasna his tree. It was oor tree."

"Aye. But will he no get hame again, Elspie?"

Elspeth sat up in bed, her long curls falling down from her nightcap. "He disna desairve to! What gars ye speir at the man, Susan? They are a low nasty common family, and we shouldna demean oorsels by thinkin' on them."

"I dinna ken," said Su, and sobbed, "but I didna like hearin' o't." She burrowed her face into the pillow. There was a prickly feeling in her mind, as though things weren't fitting. As though she weren't, after all, part of the others. Her thoughts began to come more into English, and with different words in them. There was this word "democracy" that had been floating around in their own war, and she hadn't thought about it, but it had got in somehow, and it seemed to mean that you mustn't knock people around because they were poor. That was —that was being like Hitler. But Hitler wasn't even alive yet.

She rolled round. Elspeth was asleep. And at that she

began to think in a horror, that grew worse and worse, how from her own time all these people were dead, and Elspie there was a dead corpse, and Mysie and Helen and all, and here she was left alone with them and she could not bear it, and she slipped quickly out of bed. Here was the room that used to seem so nice and cosy with the glow of the fire and the white linen on the feather beds, and each bed tented with bright curtains into a soft cave for two yellow heads whispering over the day; it was frightening now, it was not properly there! A hundred years on, that part of the house had been pulled about and altered and made into cupboards, and there was a bathroom there with taps, and that was real. Taps and the white enamel bath that you turned on yourself. That was real.

Her clothes were there, lying on a stool in the firelight. She put them on. Chemise and petticoats that tied behind, and her day dress of cinnamon wool with India muslin trimmings. It fastened in front with a pearl brooch, and she jagged herself with the hurry she was in. For a moment she stood with her pricked finger in her mouth and her eyes screwed up. When she opened them again, the Brounie was standing on the far side of the hearthrug. "There's a good wee lassie," he said. "Haste ye noo, for your boy is clean scared oot o' his skin, and him standin' there in the night."

"Oh!" said Su. "Is it—*please*, is it Winkie?"

"Aye, aye, and terrible eydent to be seein' ye, and wonderin' how in a' the world your folks hae been sae hard on his."

"But what have we done?"

"There is a wild bing o' blood atween ye the noo, lassie, but ye'll be hearing frae hissell. Gae hooly noo! Ye'll no' need tae wake the lave o' the hoose." The Brounie went ahead of her, half turning, and there seemed to be a nice wee handful of green light in the palm of his hand that he held behind him, so that she could see her way out of the room and down. They went softly past the dining-room door. Inside the gentlemen were roaring with laughter and banging on the table, and once there was the small sharp tinkle of broken glass. They came to the side door, that had the bar up across it, but when the Brounie lifted his hand, the bar gave a kind of soft oily grunt and pushed back, and the door opened a crack. Outside it was moonlight, and ivy leaves stirring across it. Su took one step, and then another. She looked round. And there, a few feet away along the wall, was Winkie, his body pressed into the ivy, his hands gripping, and in the moonlight he was looking so horribly frightened that Su ran to him. He seemed to shrink in closer to the wall, and he was saying something in the Gaelic. "Winkie," she whispered, and shook him. Then, quick, his hands came up to her own, and he spoke in English, but with a kind of awkwardness. Yet that went away after a few sentences. "Is it you at last?" he said. "Och, Su, is it truly you?"

"Sure as you're there," said Su. "Oh, Winkie, what is the matter?" For Winkie had both arms round her neck, and he was hugging her tight, and his face was against her neck, with his lips dry and his eyes wet. It wasn't like Winkie at all. He never used to be soppy. It was uncomfortable being held so hard, but he seemed awfully upset, so she wanted to be nice to him. "Winkie dear," she said, "what on earth is it?"

He said, very low, "I thought you had forgotten, Su. I thought you would be for ever in the Big House, and me where I am. Oh Su."

She kept hold of him. He was wearing some kind of an old shirt, made of very coarse stuff; it was hard under her hands, but the awful thing was that his shoulders under it seemed to be so thin and bony, different from what they

46

used to be. He had breeches of a kind, torn round his knees, and his feet and legs were bare. "Why didn't you come before, Winkie?" she said.

"I was wanting to find you," he said, "but how could I? I saw you at the kirk, and whiles you seemed to be keeking round for me. But I and my folks were aye away at the back, and yours in the front, and I daredna gie you a straight look, even."

"Oh Winkie, why not?"

"My folks gets thrashed if they're insolent," said Winkie. "I came over to the house early on, and your coachman gave me a slashing."

"But, Winkie, there's always a whole lot of people from the village coming in and out."

"Ach yes, they're the tame ones, but my lot arena' liked any at the Big House, the way we have been reading what it says about France and freedom, and there was one or two had a wee bit siller put by, so they didna have to gang on their knees to your lot. But now—now my cousin Dougie's been caught, and they gave him a terrible slashing and tied him up and sent him off to be killed in the Army. And—and it was your folks did that on us, Su!"

She held him tightly. "Buck up, Winkie," she said. "Don't snivel down my neck. Come on into the woods and tell me everything that happened to you from the beginning."

Chapter IV

WHAT HAPPENED TO WINKIE

———————————————

From where they were they could see the bright streaks of light between the dining-room curtains, and hear the loud feckless laughter and bursts of singing from the gentlemen passing the evening. There had been dancing earlier on, between dinner and late supper, and now the ladies were mostly asleep, or else, to judge by a lighted window up above, two or three were gossiping in their room while a servant lassie put by the dresses and laces and brushed their ringlets out. But Su and Winkie were far from all that, unspied from the house.

"I wish you had thought to bring me out a piece," said Winkie, looking at the window.

"Why," said Su, "are you hungry?"

"My wame's never full these days," said Winkie.

"I wish I'd known," said Su, worried. "They'd never miss it any in the kitchen if one took the whole of a gigot."

"Tak' a keek in your pooch, lassie!" said the Brounie, and tugged at the string of Su's swinging pocket. She looked. There was a round of shortbread in it, the same that the cook had been baking that morning with pounds of butter in it. She handed it to Winkie, who gave her a quick look, and stuck his teeth into it.

What happened to Winkie

"*You* must have put it there," said Su to the Brounie. "Then you will be his helper forby being the helper of the Big House?"

The Brounie grinned. "What for no'? Yon laddie is far oot kin o' yours on the mither's side, for a' she married a wild Macrae from up north. In this time his name is the same as your ain."

"Much good it's done me," said Winkie. "But for this," he added, licking the last crumbs of the shortbread off his fingers. "So there is the way you have been eating, Su. Well, well, it is fine to be at the Big House, surely."

"Don't be a pig, Winkie," said Su. "I never chose where I was going."

"Neither did I myself," said Winkie, "and gif I had known—but I didna. Well, will I tell you it all?" She nodded. It was queer being with him again, and not with Elspeth and the others and all their ploys together. Being just theirselves now, they were both of them back to the speech they had used 140 years on. "I opened my eyes," he said, "and it was not your hands I was holding to, and not any person's hands. I was holding on to the handles of a kind of sled, full of sea tangle, that I was hauling up from the bay, and I was that tired I had shut my eyes, and when I opened them again I had a long haul ahead of me, and a cruel pain in my arms and all over. But I knew I was needing to haul yon sled up to the field, and then back again to the bay, and the same for the whole of the day. If we had the tangle we could grow our potatoes. If we didna get it, then neither would we get our crop. Do you ken that up at the Big House, Su? There is no way out of it."

"Su, we have been working away all these weeks, and never a half-day on the Saturday, and whiles I would forget entirely who I was in yon world where you and I went to the school together. When I thought back on it

49

at nights I could hardly believe it was possible. It seemed like a thing that could never happen. Me going to the school and getting all kinds of learning."

"But there is a school in these times," said Su. "I know, because I heard my granny speaking of it."

"But do you ken what like of a school it is? It is a school for wee ones to learn to speak the English and say their catechism, and they are strapped if they speak the Gaelic. And the older lassies stay on, and are taught to spin and weave and sew, and the school sells what they make, and they get nothing, and then they are taken on as servants in the big houses. It is yon sort of a school, Su. It is a school for slaves!"

"But Winkie, how awful. I don't believe my granny can know it is like that."

"She knows just fine," said Winkie. "But she is wanting to keep us down, the same as the rest of you. And the very same as the minister himself, who teaches the catechism, and who needs to keep the right side of the heritors, and pleased as a spaniel if he is asked up to dinner at the Big House! But I can tell you a thing, Su. They teach us the English in the school, the way we will not be consoling ourselves with our own songs and stories in the Gaelic, and the way the minister can preach at us and we will have to understand. But if you can read the English catechism, then you can read the pamphlets by the United Scotsmen. Do you ken what that is, Su?" Su shook her head. "They are the ones that will get us freedom—and votes—and no' to be put out of our houses when the laird says. Su, there's estates up north where the lairds have put out every living man and woman that is in it, and packed them all off like beasts to Canada and yon wild parts. They are putting in sheep instead of folk, but the sheep's wool will never go to clothe the ones that used to live in the houses where the sheep shelter. It is not so here, Su, not yet, because my lot are fishing as well as crofting, and havena so much land to be coveted by yon King Davids. But it is in your folks' power to do the same thing, and we will not bear it! And the army is the laird's thing, Su, and they could be firing on the folk in Glasgow or Kilmarnock that is wanting liberty and down with the kings and oppressors, and now they have taken Dougie for a soldier, Su, and he was awful nice, and I will never-ever see him any more!"

"Oh Winkie, don't!" said Su. "All this we're in, it isn't real." She looked round for the Brounie, but he was away. It didn't matter. She'd got Winkie back.

"Maybe yours isna, but mine is. It's real, Su, right enough. And Dougie had made me a whistle and he was just after making me a wee boat, and now he is gone, and his mother greeting terrible, and all for one old tree."

"Stop it!" said Su. "You've got to tell me what happened to you from the day you got here. Did you go to this school?"

"Nae fears," said Winkie. "I was working."

"How?"

"Well, I was herding, and helping every which way on the croft, and baiting lines. Su, there's far more fishing in the bay now than in our time. That will be with the trawlers not coming. But the boats is awful wee, and never an engine to any of them. And the nets are wee, and so is the price you get for the fish. Still and all, I was at the school when I was a bairn, Su, because I can read the English. Mostly I canna speak it so plain as I am doing now, but it is us being together. The old words come back."

"Can you write and do sums?"

"Well, I just dinna know, Su, and there's the fact. There was no paper and pencils in it. And if we were hauling up the tangle, well, it just had to cover the field, however many loads that might be. And we couldna get running off at five o'clock. Did you have school, Su?"

"Well, I have lessons, but I don't believe it was ever sums. Even in the big kitchen there aren't any weights. It is all done by eye. I never thought of that before."

"There was the way my uncle would look at a field, or my cousin Neilie would judge what cloth he needed for a stand of clothes. Oh Su, Neilie is fair heart-broken over Dougie. He was terrible fond of him altogether, and so was I."

"Go on with what you have been doing, Winkie," said Su firmly, putting an arm round him.

"Well, it was mostly working, but there would be evenings we would be up at Neilie's and talking away about all that was going on, and me listening. Or there would be a bit *ceilidh* in one house or another. But there is no wireless."

"No, of course there isn't. It isn't invented yet."

"Well, to be honest with you, Su, I hadna mind on it till this minute. And I used to be forever turning it on and off. Maybe the singing is bonnier."

"Did you dance? We danced a lot."

"Aye. On a Saturday night, mostly, but I was awful tired at nights. I slept on straw, Su. It was awful scratchy the times I didna sleep straight away. But mostly I did. We had only the one room, and little enough in it, and all the cooking done on the hearth, and most of the light coming from the hearth forby. But it could be cheery. I spoke with the piper all the same—our own piper, Donul Beg. And he kind of half knew me. It was one night up at Neilie's house, and first Neilie had been reading aloud from a newspaper. It was called the *Morning Chronicle*. It was a Whig paper, and there were bits in it against the Lairds. There'd been another paper, Su, called *Pig's Meat*, and do ye ken for why? That was because of yon man

What happened to Winkie

Burke that called us swine, aye, a swinish multitude! How would you like that now, Su? Neilie had *The Rights of Man* in under a roll of tweed, and the trials of Muir and Margarot and the rest that yon wicked judge Braxfield had jailed and transported. And when he read out a piece, then Dougie and my uncle would be speaking about it, and wondering what like folk were in England and France and all these wild places. Dougie was making me a wee boat, and her sails made out of cuttings of stuff, awful nice, Su, and—och, he never finished it."

"Well, then, in came the Clan Ferguson. Right enough, Donul Beg's brothers were all big men grown, but not one had the same music as Donul. So he was playing, and the rest listening and speaking of the stories that went with the tunes. And one of them had a snuff mull that he passed around once in a while, and after a bit Neilie took out the bottle from the press, and they had a dram all round. But from the way they spoke, I think the Clan Ferguson had maybe had a refreshment already that evening, or maybe two, for Donul had been playing at a wake on one of the far-out crofts. It had been a good-going funeral, so they said, for the grandfather there had siller put by, and had given orders for its spending on the day he died. So there was Donul with the stuff lighting him up grand for the playing. And I was half asleep, Su, and half listening with the queer dreams coming shuddering through me on the pipe music, and all of a sudden the piper made a grab at me."

"I mind I stood before him, Su, and he with a grip of my shirt, and myself blinking, and my bare feet in the edge of the warm peat ash on the hearth. He looked at me long, and his breath had a comforting smell off it of good whisky. He said to me, 'I have seen you before this.' You will mind, Su, we were speaking in the Gaelic. And the rest laughed and said Aye, surely, I was wee Winkie from up-by. But he shook his head as though the midges had been at him, and he said, 'It is not that at all!' Then he said, 'Where is your lassie?' The rest laughed terrible, and myself feeling so affronted I could have bitten him. And then he said slow, 'Aye, she is up at the Big House.' Neilie said, 'Are you after one of the servant lassies already, and you no older than a twig?' I didna know what to answer at all, but the piper said, 'It is no servant lassie. But a Big House lassie it is.' Then the rest told him to give over. He was talking foolishly, and it was trouble he would be bringing on himself and me and all of them, and he had drunk one dram too many. But my mind was waking up inside me, and I thought of you, Su, and all we have to do yet, and it seemed queer to be thinking on you up there at the House and me where I was. And then the piper said, 'It is not the drink. It is the Sight.'

"Then they all looked terrible put about, as though he had said a bad word, and they tried to speak of other things, but he kept a grip on me, and he said, 'What was it you were wanting to ask me, laddie?' So I said, 'Tell me where is the way to the Hill, for I have not found it.' And that was true enough, Su, for I had looked plenty times when I was up herding, and there was no sign of it that I could see, not even on Knocnashee. The others were laughing a bit at my question, but I could see all the same that they were yet more put about, and I was feared I might get a skelping over it. But he nodded his head, and he said, 'There are as many doors to the Hill as there are doors to the house of the field mouse, and full as hard to see. But when the time comes, my son, go you down by the Seal Rock, and that door will take you in as surely as the door on Knocnashee. But hand-in-hand you must go.'

"He had a sort of queer look on him yet, so I thought I would dare to ask one question more. I said, 'How will I find the lassie of the Big House?' And he said—well, I dinna hardly like saying it, Su, but he said, 'I can see the lassie.' And he said that twice, Su, as though he was seeing sure enough, and the others stayed gey still. And then he said, 'It is your folks have been at her, laddie, and sore and sad they have left her. Ach, the poor lassie!' And then Neilie the tailor said, 'Will that be the revolution, Donul?' But the piper shook his head and he said, 'No, it is not that. Oh no.' And then, Su—then he gave a kind of a start, and a scunnered look came on him, and he let go of me and then he gave a wee sort of laugh as though he were wanting to excuse himself for having said what he shouldna, and he scratched in his beard and spat into the fire. And then one of his brothers said they must be getting home surely."

"After the Fergusons were gone, nobody spoke of the matter, and they seemed to act in an over-polite way towards myself, as though I were a stranger. And the next day I was made to drink some terrible nasty, bitter stuff. It is my belief, Su, they thought I was bewitched some way. They made me jump three times over a fire, and I have rowan berries round my neck yet. But I never got skelped. Su, you arena fashing yourself over yon thing he said about yourself? Maybe it wasna true at all."

"But it's happened already," said Su, "at least it's going to. At least—oh Winkie, you silly goof, can't you see it's me at Hallowe'en and all those beasts from the school?"

"Well, aren't you the clever one, Su! I never thought, but that will be it. Of course. And if that was true, maybe the rest will be true."

"About the Seal Rock," said Su, frowning. "That's where Colin's house is in our time—isn't it?"

"Aye, but how are we to get there? If your folk caught me now, they'd half kill me."

"Oh Winkie, I'm sure you've got it all mixed up. They

can't be like that. I know they wouldn't punish anyone unless they did something wrong."

"Was it that wrong to cut a tree when my folk needed wood so desperate for every kind of patching and mending, and keeping the wind and rain out of the house?"

"But there must have been something else."

"Aye, so there was. It was the thoughts in the heads of my lot. And maybe if Dougie had gone with his bonnet in his hand and begged for the wood he might have been let take it. But he isna that kind."

"I suppose he was a poacher, too. Just the same as your own real father, Winkie!"

"Och, Su!" said Winkie, and gave her a dig in the ribs. "You shouldna be listening to tales. How often have I told you? My own father hasna taken so much as would make a meal, not since the keeper went and your mother went to work down at the war in London, and you came to the school. And fine you know it. It is only the tinks that's poaching now."

"Aye, Ian Townsley said he would take me out one night."

"What are you saying, Su? You canna go with the tinks! You're a wee devil, that's what you are. Och, Su, are you sure all this isna taking time out of our real lives? It seems terrible like time going by now, and when we are speaking of our real lives I canna help wondering when I will be home again."

"Well, I am almost sure it is all right," said Su. "But it's awfully muddling. I think we shan't understand until we get back. I suppose, Winkie, people in this time have got to poach for food, but in our real lives it's all come to be kind of light, like a game one's playing at."

"Ach, yes, it's just to pass the time. If it werena that way my father wouldn't be making his jokes in front of you."

"I always liked that. It made me feel kind of—in the game you were playing."

"Did you, Su? Honest, do you like coming to our house?"

"You know I do, Winkie."

"Ach, well, I just didna know right. And my father was aye saying he was terrible sorry for you, up there alone in the Tigh Mór. But we didna rightly know. It could have been some way a rudeness wanting you to come. Well, we'll know now. If we ever get back. Will we get back, Su, are you sure?"

"Of course I'm sure, Winkie. The Brounie will take care of us some way. And—you never finished, Winkie."

"About Dougie, is it? Well—Su, if you think you can go out with the tinks, will you come with me this night and help us get vengeance for Dougie?"

"O.K., Winkie. How?"

He whispered close to her ear. "On your uncle."

Su looked round quick. It was as though there were listeners in every bush. "Winkie," she said, "you can't!"

"We can, so," said Winkie, and then, with a wild anxiety on him, "Su, you will not go in and speak of it at the House?"

"You aren't going to kill him?" she asked, feeling terribly worried and some way responsible.

"Na, na," said Winkie, "that wouldna do. Though I would like it fine. But we will set on him, Su, and have him off his horse, and give him a slashing, the same as he gave Dougie, and Neilie said I could come with him, the way I was the one that liked Dougie so well. Neilie and I, we have both got kind of false-faces, so folk won't know us. We are to catch him on the brae when he goes by the night."

"But will he go by? I didn't know."

"There is one of the ghillies has slipped the word,"

said Winkie. "Now, will you come, Su, or is it only talk?"

She said, "They'll spot me, Winkie."

"Not in the dark. It is all rocks and bushes there, and nobody need see. And you canna go back into the house now, Su. It's been so terrible long for me, you don't know. Ach, Su, now we are the two of us together, let's stay. Dinna go back! I have hated yon house. Dinna make me hate it more."

"O.K.," said Su, "I'll come."

He jumped to his feet and pulled her up. In among the bushes here she had so nearly got back to how she used to be, that she began to run properly, with long steps, and tripped over her skirt. They had to go slower. She took off the silly little kid slippers and went barefoot, as indeed she and Elspie often did outside when the grown-ups weren't looking. Once they were out of sight of the house they went slowly where the moonlight showed there was grass underfoot, but they only spoke in whispers. Su was more worried than she let on to Winkie. She knew that what they were at was likely to bring the worst kind of consequences, that if it were known who did it, her own family would destroy the guilty ones. She began to remember one thing after another that had been said at table about the behaviour of the lower classes, rebelliousness and Jacobinism and anarchy. And wasn't this ploy they were on the worst kind of all three? She remembered hearing and not heeding at the time how other big families had responded to crimes against them by their tenants. And her own lot had applauded it. She began to try and tell Winkie. To tell him how, if he was recognized, his lot would be wiped out, root and branch. Their houses would be taken from them. They would be put in prison, and maybe transported. But it appeared that Winkie knew this, and that Neilie the tailor and he were disregarding it because of the anger and grief that were on them. And the more Su said what might happen, the more Winkie's anger grew against the Big House. At last she stopped saying it. She began to reason that the Brounie must have meant her to go, or he would not have led her down the stairs and out past the cold iron of the door-bars. And she began to think also of the thing the piper had said to her about the duty of the Big House ones to have courage.

She needed to have courage. It was frightening going through the woods and across the stepping stones. Winkie was so angry he didn't mind, but she was only anxious. On the far side they went up on to the road that was only two cart ruts and grass growing between them. And here they hid behind a rock, and Winkie tied a strip of dark cloth over his nose and cheeks, so that he wouldn't be known. And then in a bit there was someone whistling two bars of a tune from across the road, and Winkie answered it and left her by the stone, and went over. In a while he came back. He had the end of a cart-rope in his hand, and he tied it on to one of the stunted oaks beside the rock so that it was about a foot above the road. Su began to feel awfully bothered about the horse. She tried to say something, but Winkie laughed in the nasty way he had laughed that time in real life when Su had told him he was a beast for blowing up puddocks with straws. He finished tying the rope and came over, feeling for where she was in the black shadow. Then they stayed crouched in beside the stone, and Winkie was shivering a good bit. Su put her arm round him, and suddenly felt the hilt of the piper's sgian in under the belt of his breeches.

Chapter V

MY HANDS TO WAR

"Winkie," said Su urgently, "Winkie!" But he was not heeding. It was simply awful being there with one's head full of things that ought to be said, and Winkie gone off into a kind of hard daze. What was happening back at the house? Supposing Elspie woke up? What at all could she tell Elspie? And then she began to realize that this must be the beginning of the adventure that she had come into the past to have, and she was very unlikely ever to see Elspie again. And they had planned such a lovely party in the play-house. Princess Perdita, who was the biggest of the lady dolls, and who had a French lace cap and apron and an ivory fan that really opened and shut, was going to have twins, and they were going to have a christening party. They had made the twins and put them into the play-house bed. And perhaps she wouldn't be there for it, Su thought. Oh, bother, bother, bother! And then, a good long way off yet, there was a horse coming up the road. "Are you sure he'll be alone?" she whispered. Winkie nodded. Now she could hear the breathing of the horse as he came to the steep part of the hill.

She knew the horse would stumble in a minute. She began to ache all down her legs with the thought of the horse. She couldn't really see the man on the horse; he had a cloak with a broad riding hat. Her uncle had been horrid about poor people, just the same way Winkie had been horrid about the puddocks. She could smell the horse, she could hear the creak of the leather on it. Now!

The horse stumbled but did not come down. Then there was a yell from the far side, and the rider was swearing and slashing down with his whip, and Winkie had run in under it and caught the bridle. Neil must be pulling her uncle off at the far side—he had dropped his cloak. She could see his arm up and the black whip against the moon. It seemed as if he must be winning, he would slash the tailor off and get away, or turn on the two of them. The horse, held hard, was pawing and snorting. Winkie put his hand down to the knife, and cut through curb and snaffle. The horse threw up his head and started forward as Winkie jumped back and clear. The rider, thrown off his balance, slithered and fell heavily backward, and came down with the other two on top of him. He was fighting hard, though, and suddenly there was the crack of a pistol going off, and Su yelped. She had run out from the rock wondering what in all the world she could do. She kept on saying, "Oh don't, oh don't!" She could hear herself saying it, but nobody paid any attention. The other man was trying to pummel her uncle's face, and Winkie was holding on to his right arm, but was off his own feet and flung about every which way like a terrier hanging on to a bull. Suddenly, Su saw the pistol on the ground, with a trickle of smoke coming out of the barrel, and her uncle's hand reaching for it. She ran in and picked it up. She was awfully afraid it would go off, so she pointed it the other way into the wood, holding it with both hands, and one hand caught on something, and it did go off, jumping in her hands in an awfully nasty way. She put it down behind the rock. She was crying a little. She didn't want to look. She wanted to be back in bed with Elspie.

Suddenly Winkie was there. "Run, Su!" he said. "They've heard the shots."

She ran as hard as she could, dragging her silly skirts up over her knees. They were on a grass path going down, not too bad to run on. The man who was holding on to Winkie's other hand must be Neilie the tailor. He was saying something in the Gaelic she couldn't understand; she was out of breath, she had a stitch in her side, a thorn in her foot. Who was after them, anyway?

Suddenly Winkie gave a sharp tug at her hand, pulling her right round into the wood, which was thicker here, for now they were in the lee of the small glen that went down to the sea. They ducked between hazels and under a fallen tree-trunk, clammy with moss. "Where's Neil?" whispered Su, gasping for breath, nursing her foot.

"He went on," answered Winkie. "He saw I couldn't run so fast as himself. He will draw them off."

"Oh," said Su, "oh—*we* ought to have done that. Will he get caught, Winkie?"

"I dinna think," said Winkie. "He knows the lie of the land."

"Would he see me?"

"He didna say, Su. Aye, by jings, he did! But he thought—och, he thought you were a fairy, Su! Indeed, now that I've mind of what he said, he thought you were my Guardian. Wasna that a daft notion, Su?"

"Well, I might be," said Su. "I kind of half am. I got that pistol away, Winkie."

"What garred you let it off, Su? It was yon two shots that set folks after us."

"I couldn't help it," said Su, "it went off by itself."

"Guns dinna do that," said Winkie scornfully.

"They do with me," said Su, and then, "Quiet, there's someone coming."

Two men came running down the path. One was a man Su had sometimes seen about the house. They stopped almost opposite the fallen tree, turning and speaking to one another, as though they hardly knew what to do. A moment afterwards Su's uncle came up, on his horse, the cut reins knotted on to the bridle. His hat was off, and in the moonlight they could see blood on his face. He shouted angrily at the men in English, asking them if they were going to let two ruffians get away. One of the men answered that they would know soon enough in the morning who was missing, and would get them that way. Every house and hut would be searched, they said, and any with a mark on them taken up to be questioned at the Big House. The uncle said fiercely that there would be the mark of a lash on one of them, and gave a crack with his whip that made Su and Winkie jump and hold on to one another. Then he said that he knew fine one of them would be out of the house of Neil the tailor —"Aye, maist like the villain himself. We'll see gin he be marked. And by God gin it be sae, as I weel jalouse, its worse marked he'll be, and weel hangit at the end o't!"

One of the men seemed to ask something, for the uncle answered more angrily than ever, "Aye, twa men o' them it was!" And then he wheeled the horse and went plunging back up the glen. In a while the men looked at one another and turned and followed him.

"Did you hear?" whispered Winkie. "Two men! Did you see me cut the reins, Su?"

"Yes," said Su unkindly, "it was awfully silly. The horse might have killed you."

"No' me," said Winkie, "I was fly enough for that. If I hadna—oh Su, did he mean it, yon about hanging Neilie?"

"Yes," said Su. "Oh yes. Winkie, we've got to find Neil and warn him. He mustn't go home."

"But he had on a false-face."

"People aren't such fools as you think. My uncle's bound to suspect Neil. Oh, I do wish you hadn't."

"It was just grand thrashing him," said Winkie, "but maybe you're right, Su. We will need to try and find Neilie."

They came out cautiously. Su's frock was wringing wet and she had dropped her shoes. Winkie was beginning to feel his bruises. They went on down. The scrub oak and hazel lightened. They could hear the seuch of the sea in front of them, and in a moment they could see it, calm beyond the rocks, with the diamond path, the great and ancient road of the moon, clear across it, ahead of them. Now there was coarse sand under foot. Looking carefully, Winkie found a footmark. "He will have gone down the way," he said. "Come on, Su, I will give the signal in a bit." They went on. After a while Winkie whistled the two bars, but got no answer.

"Where are we at all?" Su asked.

"Near the Seal Rock," said Winkie; and then, "Su, that is where the way into the Hill is!"

"Well, we can't go till we've found Neil," said Su. The moon was low in the sky. Su suddenly found herself yawning. "Let's sit down a minute," she said. "My feet are awful sore."

"O.K.," said Winkie. "But not for long, mind you." He reached down and put his hand on one of Su's feet. "Your feet will be soft, Su. Mine's is awful hard. Are you hungry, Su?"

"No," she said. "But—oh, I do wish it was all finished and I was back in bed." She leant her head against the rock behind her and shut her eyes. Her head was buzzing. It seemed to her that the buzzing began to take a shape, began to be singing. She listened to it in an increasing contentment. Suddenly Winkie was poking at her, saying they should be getting on. She opened her eyes; it had been a nice dream. But she could hear it still, and louder. "Listen!" she said.

It was louder every minute, as though somewhere folk were singing, tossing their voices into the air like silver and golden balls, the tunes weaving richly through one another. It wasn't only voices, it was instruments, bells, flutes, tinkling, twangling, sounds and sweet airs that give delight but hurt not. "What is that one we hear now, Winkie?" she whispered.

"It's like a melodeon," he whispered, "but it isna. It is too light some way."

"It sounds as if it were somewhere quite close, just behind a curtain," she whispered back, and stood up and edged round the corner of the great rock. "Here!" she said, and reached back her hand for Winkie.

They were standing on the lowest step of three stone steps that led up to a doorway, the door of which was half open, and a steady soft light behind it and beyond that the music and a smell that was hawthorn and whin flowers in spring sunshine, and baking bread. Su went up another step. "It's the door of the Hill right enough," said Winkie, and he lifted one hand to his neck and gave a tug, and the rowan berries pattered down on to the stone.

"Come on," said Su, and went up to the third step and then stopped and dropped Winkie's hand. "Oh Winkie," she said, "we've forgotten about Neil!"

Winkie was looking at the door. He said, "Are you sure we can do anything, Su? I mean—folk coming out of one time canna change what happened in another. That's sure. And—och, Su, I want to get back. I've had enough and plenty of this time."

Su said, "I know it ought to be like that. I don't be-

65

lieve we could alter history. But this isn't exactly history, Winkie. It isn't battles and dates. It is just—someone. I think it would be kind of dishonourable to leave him now, Winkie."

"Well," said Winkie, "just as you say, Su. But I'm awful keen to get back." He looked at her. The music kept on calling. She shook her head.

"Well," he said, "I'll try once more." It was gey difficult to whistle his own tune against yon other, the fairy tune. He could not do it at all on the steps. He needed to go right away and stand out on the shingle. He whistled the two bars and waited. And this time the whistle was answered.

Su watched from the steps. She saw a man come out from the shadows between the rocks further along and go over to Winkie, who caught hold of him, speaking quick in the Gaelic. After a bit she said, "What's up, Winkie?" Winkie came over, half pulling the man with him. Su was looking at him; he had a short beard, and was wearing ordinary working clothes, the coat muddy and torn at the neck.

Winkie said, "*Tha e*—och, Su, my words is all tapsalteery! He is saying he will get to Kilkieran, and then he'll leave the country for a while till the thing's blown by."

"It's a long way," said Su, "and my lot will have men out along all the roads by morning."

"Aye, I'm thinking that. He said I should go with him. I canna explain, Su."

"He had best come into the Fairy Hill," said Su.

The man took his bonnet out of his pocket, put it on, and then took it off again, and bowed to Su. "If it is the English that is spoken by the Bean-shith", he said, "then it is the English that Neil, son of Hamish, will be speaking. And indeed we will come with you, mistress, for it is an ill taking we are in, surely."

My Hands to War

"I'm not a fairy," said Su anxiously.

"Just as you say, mistress, just as you say," said Neil.

"Take my hand, Winkie," said Su, "and hold on to him—and—and I am almost sure we'll be all right."

She put her free hand up to the door. It swung inward on a touch, and the three of them crossed the threshold. Behind them the door closed just as softly. They were in a high vaulted cave. You could not even see the roof, and the floor was soft. Su's toes tried to determine whether it was fine sand or a pale gold carpet. It was not certain from what source the light was coming, nor whether the walls were of rock stained with drip and mosses, or painted with ancient pictures. At the far end was a curtain, and the music coming more strongly from behind it. Winkie grabbed at Su. "Wait you, we'll need to think what to do!"

"How can we?" said Su. "We don't know what it will be like; and, anyway, whatever you do, Winkie, I've got to meet the King of Babylon." And she smoothed down her wet, crumpled dress and walked through the curtain.

As she did it, the delightful and triumphant singing had changed to a *port a beul*, unimaginably wild and sweet and birdlike, a fluttering of nonsense words. She had always wanted to dance to a *port a beul*. It had always seemed silly sitting through them at concerts. And now in an instant she was dancing to it, in a double eightsome, and on one side her partner was Winkie, whose hand she still held, but on the other it was that same Prince of the Fair People whom she had seen last in the library of the Big House.

She found herself terribly, wildly glad. He had been lost, and now he was found. And there, yes, there on a kind of platform that was covered with white sheepskins and great heaps of golden whin branches was the beautiful hound with the gold collar sitting on his haunches with

67

his tongue out, grinning dog-fashion at Su. It was her turn
to go into the ring of the dancing. She looked down at
her dress, all messy and dull among the shining ones. But
the Prince swept down over it with his hand, and a queer
tingling feel went with the touch, and she was wearing a
dress like her green party frock, but splashed with silver
stars and belted with silver set opals. And when she set to
Winkie, he was wearing a ruffled shirt and a kilt of the
tartan that was her own and his on the mother's side, and
the belt on it like hers. The dance partner whose other
hand he had been holding was a golden-haired girl, who
looked at Su with bright eyes, as though she were sharing
a secret. Her dress was soft and swirling green, and in her
hair were tassels of flowers of several colours. But it was
not so clear whether these flowers were real and unfading
or carved out of jewels. Neil the tailor was dancing in the
same set, and he, too, was wearing the tartan that she knew
well. Until the dance ended, she need not think nor plan.
No action was to be taken. The *port a beul* came now from
one part of the hall, now from another. From the great
circles of the first reel they broke into foursomes. The
singing changed time from reel to strathspey and back
again. When Su was dancing with the fairy girl, there was
something about it that set her off into great mouthfuls of
laughing, and Winkie seemed to be the same. Suddenly
it ended.

Cups were being passed round from hand to hand, deep
goblets of patterned gold and flat quaichs with twisted
handles, and whatever the drink it was cool and swirling
in them. She knew it would taste like strawberry ices and
real apricots and oranges. The smell and freshness were
close to her lips. Then she remembered. "Winkie," she
cried, "don't drink!"

Immediately the Fair People were round them. She felt
she had committed some dreadful rudeness. Trying to

excuse it, she said, "We have got to see Neil is all right first!"

"That we will do surely," said the Prince, and then he spoke to Neil. "What do you wish to see?" He had a small round mirror in his hands. As he spoke he stretched it like a sheet of silk until it was the full stretch of his arms. Neil and the children looked in it. It was no surprise to any of the three of them that it did not reflect themselves. But at last there seemed to be a square shape in the bottom of it. This became larger. It was a door. The mirror became brighter. The door opened into a bare room, with a bench along one side of it, and a dozen men sitting on the bench, wearing red coats and dark kilts. There were muskets piled together in one corner, their butt-ends on the floor; a couple of belts were slung over the top of them, and another lay on the floor. Most of them looked sad enough, and one or two had their heads in their hands. But two were drinking out of a bottle, and seemed to be singing, though no sound came out of the mirror. And then one of the sad ones lifted his head and stared straight at them, and Neil and Winkie both cried out that it was Dougie.

"What is your wish?" said the Prince gently to Neil, and Neil lifted his head, with the tears running down from his eyes into his beard.

"I wish I was with my decent poor brother," he said. "Aye, even though it means I am to go as a sodger."

"Go to him, then," said the Prince.

Neil turned to Winkie. "You will be fine here, laddie?" he said questioningly. "Och, yes indeed, I can see you are fine. Well, I will be leaving you now." So at that he stepped over the rim and into the mirror, and it swallowed him up. And the Prince drew his arms together until the mirror was again small and round between his two hands.

"And now", said the Prince to Su, "you will eat and

drink with us?" And again the cups were brought and the golden ashets of cake and fruit, all perfect of their kind.

"Do you know", said Su, in her best grown-up voice, "I am really not hungry just now."

"Winkie is hungry," said Winkie's lovely partner. "Eat now! Do you think I would harm you, Winkie? Do you think it is in me to harm you?" And she smiled at him.

Su snatched at his hands. "Don't eat, Winkie. Remember!"

"It seems", said the Prince of the Fair People, in a clear even voice, from which they could tell nothing, "that we need to take you before the King."

"Yes," said Su. "Oh yes, I am sure you'd better."

They moved out of the dance hall, Winkie dragging behind, but Su with a grip of him. The curtain fell between themselves and the music. For a time they were in darkness. As it lifted, they became aware that there was a burn flowing through the vaulted cave they were in, and they were going downward beside it on a sand path. Both began to see fishes, and nudged one another. These were not ordinary brown trout, but many coloured, and some had the most entrancing and amusing shapes, which might have been ugly if the fish had been dead and still, but they were not, but for ever moving and catching the light and making unexpected appearances. The children went slower and slower, glancing round at the Prince, but he did not seem to mind. He went at their pace. At last they stopped altogether. It was beyond them to go on.

The burn was now some four or five feet across, broken by rocks tufted with moss and sometimes flowers, which they half knew and half found astonishing. At the far side there seemed to be bright turf, sometimes meadowy and sometimes broken with bell heather or bog asphodel. They did not remember that they were within the Hill and that it was rightly night. This place was innocent with spring. A waterhen paddled out, followed by a string of soft babies. A water vole popped from his burrow and sat up to wash his whiskers. Su and Winkie were now kneeling on a moss-bedded rock, close to the surface of the water, and the coloured lipping fishes. The great hound lay beside them and they stroked him as they spoke in whispers. There were other water birds sailing in and out behind the rocks, brilliant and bright-eyed drakes. Wagtails poised delicately. There might have been a flamingo beyond the next bend. Now a dragonfly hovered and darted. At last a fawn came down over the green turf, its ears wide and eyes full of wonder and no enmity.

"If only we had something to give it," said Su, half aloud, and there under her hand was a piece of bread. She held it out. The fawn came nearer, stepping down into the water with one foot. Where the bread crumbled the fishes rose to take it. A duck rushed and gobbled, leaving a bubble wake. Step by step the fawn crossed through the shallow rippling water, and its long tongue came out for the bread. It ate out of her hand. Her fingers and Winkie's explored up its delicate soft muzzle, stroked round its ears. They lifted it gently out of the water on to the rock beside them. "I wonder if it will stay with us," said Su. She got up softly and moved a step away. The fawn followed and licked her hand. She had never enjoyed anything so much in her life before, and she got the straight look of delight and a sharing of happiness from Winkie. They knelt beside the wild fawn tamed among the grass and bells and flower candles and spires and all was well. They turned their mortal faces to the Prince of the Fair People.

"Well," he said, "you may keep it for yourselves." And his hand went down to stroke the great noble head of his own hound, and he smiled at them.

"Oh, may we really?" said Su. But Winkie cried out suddenly, "No, Su, we canna take gifts!"

A shiver went through everything, a cold wind, a withering of flowers, a flitting away of birds and dragon-flies, a fish belly up and stiff in the water. And the fawn dead on the ground between them.

"Oh!" cried Su. "Oh—you are *beasts*!" And she stamped and her hands clenched on the stuff of her dress. And her fingers felt it different, and she knew it, and she shouted at the Prince, "You give me back my own frock and take this away!"

"Even to go before the King of Babylon?" said the Prince, and the queer thing was he didn't seem to have minded. He wasn't angry at them as they were angry at him. He seemed kind of half sorry for them. "Will you not borrow from us, children of middle earth?" he asked.

"No," said Su, "I won't! Will you, Winkie?"

"I'll do the same as you, Su," said the boy.

Again there was a shiver over the hill, and Su found herself in the school clothes she hated most, gym tunic and jersey and thick black cotton stockings. It was what half the girls wore at the Port-na-Sgadan school, and she hadn't liked it any the better for that. And Winkie was in his grubby school clothes, and the boots that were a bit too small for him. "Oh dear," said Su, "I do wish—no, I don't."

Chapter VI

THE KING OF BABYLON

Again they went with the Prince, but the path was narrow and the water dark and empty. Neither of them looked back at the dead fawn. "Maybe it wasna real, the poor wee beastie," said Winkie, in an attempt at comfort.

"It licked my hand," said Su mournfully.

"I liked awful much wearing yon kilt and the bonny shirt," said Winkie. "I've aye thought to myself I'd look a clown in a kilt, but it didna seem that way."

"You suited them great," said Su. "Oh, I do hate school clothes. Winkie, have you got your sgian yet?"

He nodded. "They couldna take that." He would like to have whistled, but it didna seem some way right.

But now the path began to broaden out, and the waters to flatten into a dark loch. They were coming into another great hall, of which the half was still water, and here and there the leaves of the water-lily, but no blossoms yet, and the other half was smooth as glass. It was apparent that they were now in the centre of the Hill, and the light was not so bright that they could see clear from one end to another of the place, nor where the waters ended. After a time they came to a copper head on a pillar alone on a marble floor, eyeless and shining. The head began to waggle its jaw at them. They clutched on to one another. It was most awfully nasty. A clicking began inside the head and it said in a whirring voice, "Stop, mortal strangers, and answer my riddles."

"All right," said Su, and gulped.

Winkie caught hold of her and whispered, "It's all right, Su. Listen! It's kind of buzzing inside. It's a gramophone, sure enough."

"I don't think gramophones have been invented yet," said Su doubtfully.

The smooth copper jaw was waggling again. It spoke. "What is the bird that flies but is dead, and the eggs that it lays flying hatch death?"

They looked at one another. It seemed too easy. There must be a catch somewhere. The jaw began to waggle and twitch. They wanted nothing less than for it to speak again. Winkie whispered, "It must be a bomber. Try that, Su."

Su said, "We think it is a bomber."

The whirring voice said, "Sorrow, sorrow on me! Sorrow on yourselves! Children of middle earth, it is over much that you know."

"Can we go on then?" said Su shakenly.

"Go on, go on, and whatever luck you have go with you," said the head, and its jaw dropped. A rumbling sound went across the space of marble floor, and the light flickered, and thereafter seemed to have dimmed. The Prince said nothing. They both looked at the head, and it seemed to be dead, or anyway to have stopped.

"The works is run down," said Winkie. "Come on, Su!" And they made a dash past it.

Then, by the margin of the still waters they came on a man with a fishing rod. They stood and watched him, and the Prince also watched. He had bright wavy orange-fair hair, like a tinker, and a gold crown on it. His arms were bare, and as he cast they flashed with gold, for, where the Prince had one bracelet this man had two. "He looks like the king of the tinkers," whispered Su.

"He's no tink, yon!" said Winkie. "How can you say it, Su? But he is the High King, right enough."

But Su was puzzling away at it, and wondering in her mind if maybe there was some relationship between the tinkers and the fair people, although it might have been forgotten in the years between. But while she was studying away on this, the king made another cast, and down went the point of his rod, and they heard the whirr of the running tackle. They watched him play it, whispering, asking one another what fish there would be in this dark water, whether it would be one of the coloured burn fishes from the bright shallows, or maybe a great salmon or Leviathan himself. They began to see a gleam here and there, a surface boiling, a shining curve one moment above the water. At last it became apparent that he had hooked a nixie or fresh-water mermaid. She came up screaming at him, clutching at her caught hair. He stooped, picked up a handful of this hair, gave it a twist round, and slung her, yelling and flapping, bending and straightening like a fighting salmon, over his shoulder and on to a pile of silky hair and long, still arms and blue fish scales, which the children now saw on the ground behind him.

The Prince now approached him, and spoke, and the King handed him the fishing rod, which he put up. It was a great size of a rod altogether, and the flies on it of the queerest shapes and colours. The King looked at the children as though they, too, were creatures who might be thrown over his shoulder with a flick, to break on that dripping heap. In a while three or four birds with long, wavy tails trailing with sparks began to fly low round his crowned head. Su became more and more bothered about her school frock; it was all wrong; it was too short to curtsey in, and she wanted to curtsey. Instead, she just stood, and Winkie stood, kicking those tight boots of his. And the King said, "Well, mortal children, what do you seek?"

Su said, "Please, I want my shadow back."

The High King took a step towards them, and both of them felt as though they wanted to shrink up. They tried to look past him at their own Prince, but his eyes were cast down now. Yet the King spoke pleasantly and graciously. "Your shadow, is it? And where will that be now?"

Su felt baffled. She couldn't answer. But Winkie said, "You know, and we've got to have it."

"Why?" asked the King. And they both said, "To go home."

"Ach, would you leave us so soon?" asked the King. "There is nothing we cannot give you here in the Hill." And then, for a moment, a kind of foretaste of all delight came on them in breaths of sweet summer air, in a feel of rightly won reward. This was the world of all the stories they had ever really lived themselves into. This was at the back of all music, all bright colours in sunshine, all soft colours in shadow or firelight. Then Su looked at Winkie's boots, and Winkie looked at Su's gym tunic and black cotton stockings, and they didn't suit with it. And that was real. And that was home. And that was what they'd got to get back to. The delight faded, and left them with an awful feeling of grief and disappointment and regret. Out of it Winkie spoke rudely and angrily, "Give us the shadow now, and make haste with it!"

The King did not answer. Instead he asked, "What is it you want to be when you are a man, Winkie?"

Winkie, checked on this, hesitated, kicked with his boots, at last said, "Me, is it? I'm to be a fisherman."

The King of Babylon

"I can give you knowledge of herring beyond all other fishermen, Winkie. Listen!"

And at that Winkie listened, and he seemed to hear the moving of shoals through all the sounds and bays and sea lochs of Scotland; and he knew that they would be here for the spawning, and there to get the *siol-dubh*, the food that grows for them throughout summer. Yet this and that were in it to alter the ways of the herring, and fright them from the spawning grounds, or break up the spread of feed on the sea's warm surface. And here would be a shift of currents or winds, and there might be a sickness or the working of other boats, and it was only by deep knowledge, as deep as this listening, that a man might come to know the ways of the herring, and if he had this he would become known amongst the others as a lucky man, and in a short time only he would get to have a boat of his own, and from being the skipper of one he might come to have great power and respect amongst all the herring fleet. And there was what Winkie wanted most in his real life. But he said stubbornly, "I canna see what this has to do with it."

"Can you not, Winkie?" said the King. "Well then, I will ask the maiden of the Big House what it is in life she wishes."

Su said, "I don't exactly know what I want to be, only it will be someone who can stop wars happening."

The High King said, "Even the way to that is not beyond us, but it is a hard way." He took her hand, and she looked along the way, and it seemed to her to be a terrible hard way, and many of them on it were dead or dying, in some cruel and senseless fashion. And at each side there were a thousand pitfalls and temptations, and the end was beyond sight, or maybe there was no end, and indeed it was more than she had in her at this time to look along it any more.

"Please, I only want my shadow just now," she said, and she had a tired miserable feel on her, and she sniffed.

"Well," said the King, "that is a poor thin grey thing to be wanting when there are so many fine things to be had, and you would only need to ask for them, and they would be there under your hand."

"Yes," said Su, "but—but I'm unhappy without it."

"Suppose we do not choose to give it back to you?" said the King, standing over them.

"You've got to," said Winkie, "we aren't in your power." He was holding with his right hand on to the hilt of the sgian; he loosened it a little in its sheath. And yet he could not think what way to use it.

"Are you not?" said the King smiling, and Winkie, clenching his hand tightly on the hilt, felt the whole thing crumble and give, and knew that the fairy knife had acknowledged another master than himself, and his fingers met on his palm over nothing, and he was unarmed. And then he thought there was only one thing for it, and he began to whistle the tinker's tune.

At that two things happened. An utter blackness and stillness fell, and Su screamed. He reached out for her, and caught her hands, and she screamed right at his ear, but he finished the tune. Then there was nothing but darkness, and the two of them in it, and her face hot and wet with pain beside his. She was breathing very quick in gulps, and he was frightened for her. He pulled her towards him. At last she whispered, "I can't see, Winkie. Where are we?"

He whispered back, "I don't know. I suppose we are in the Hill yet. Oh Su, have they shut us in and left us?"

They were both too frightened to move. They might touch nothing but rock or earth all round, within inches of them, pressing them down to suffocate and die and be lost for ever far underground. They cowered close together. At last Su said, "Have you got your eyes shut, Winkie, or is it just all black dark?"

He said, "I think I've my eyes shut. Have you, Su?"

She said "Yes. We'd better look, Winkie."

They opened their eyes. The pendulum wagged back across the brown kitchen wall.

"Well, well," said the piper, "you havena' been long gone."

Cautiously they let go of one another. "Is it really still —then?" asked Su.

"Aye, aye," the piper said, "and now let us have a look at you, my lassie." He took her shoulders and stood her to one side of the light. "Aye, there it's," he said satisfied, "the bonny soft mortal thing! Did you have a wild job getting it out of them, my heart?"

"I never even knew I had it back," she said. "There was a terrible darkness after the tune, and an awful pain all down me."

"That will have been the shadow returning when the place of its imprisonment vanished," said the piper.

"Well, then—oh dear, the kitchen was away nicer when it was full of folk, and meat turning in front of the fire and great ashets full of everything you can think of, and cream and butter and dozens of eggs!"

"Aye," said the piper, "that will be with you yet."

"What happened to the children we were—I mean, what did people think when we disappeared?"

"Do you know that?" the piper said, turning back to the Brounie.

"Och aye," the Brounie said, "yon wee Susan that woke i' the nicht, she went back to her sleep, and she'd nae mair o' yon queer thochts, but lived douce and bairn-like for a' the years o' her bairn's life. Yet the time came on that siclike thochts were at her again. Aye aye, she was the great one for every kind o' reform, a pig-headed wee cratur, and for ever falling out wi' the lads that were after her. But there was poor folks that put their blessing on her. Aye, and she gaed into prisons and a' kinds o' low dirty places, and her own ones flyting at her. She would be helping the families o' them that were sentenced to transportation for some wee sma' theft, the like of a cotton curchie or a twa-three loaves of bread, in the bad years when the tatties failed and the corn prices went away up and folks dropped dead in the streets of Glasgow. She broke her bonny satin parasol on the heid o' a Paisley chimney sweep that had sent his laddie up a lum that was ower narrow and the laddie deed o't. She started a soup kitchen, and she made the broth hersel when the unco guid that were at it were withholding it frae those that went to the wrong kirk. Och aye, and in the end she died of a fever that came on her down Gorbals way nursing a poor woman body that had nae kin of her ain. Och, dinna greet, ye silly wee tawpie, it was a better death than most. Aye, and a better life forby."

"But was it my fault?" asked Su.

"Och no, what gars ye think sic a thing? Clean daft ye are. And as to the laddie; och aye, he went to be a sodger wi' Neilie, and baith o' them 'listed at Kilkieran, and the young fellow went as a drummie."

"But how could I have done that?" asked Winkie. "I was far ower young. I know, because there was a second cousin of mines tried to get into the Argylls after Alamein, and they wouldna let him, and he was sixteen past."

"Ither days, ither ways," said the Brounie. "Yon wee fellow liked it fine. Aye, and he liked Spain, wi' the oranges and a'. But he was killed deid at Corunna, and a wild bing o' Hielan' folks with him shot and slaughtered in nae quarrel o' their ain."

"Me killed," said Winkie, and scratched his head. "Well, well, that beats a'. But what came to Neilie and

Dougie and my poor old auntie, the mother of the two of them, that I left greeting so sore?"

"Och, weel," said the Brounie, "I needed to do some fashion o' a thing for yon poor body. I couldna' just leave her greeting her lane, since I was the guardian o' the whole lot o' ye, but it fared ill enough with the poor woman the way there was nae siller coming to the house, and the laird terrible angry at her. So she was away up the glen gathering moss litter for the kye, and greeting and yowling, and I myself was there wi' an eye on her. And at last she got a sight o' me, and I spoke to her in the Gaelic, spiering at her what way was she greeting, and here she dropped the bundle o' moss and made to grab at me, so I needed to gie a skip away and out o' her sight. And the second time she did the same, the cailleach, and it wasna till the third time that she stayed still and gied me her answer, saying it was on account o' her twa bonny sons that were lost on her. So I said to her that she was daft to greet ower twa big men and they living and cheery."

"But were they?" asked Winkie anxiously.

"Och aye, and your own Dougie a corporal. And then she gied ower greeting, and spiered at me would she see them again. So I told her the God's truth, for I told her that the t'ae she would see again, but the t'ither she wouldna see, and at yon she gied a muckle screech, and let fa' the moss, and I needing to skip. But she was right glad that the laddies were baith living, and she was blythe and bien a' the lave o' the year."

"But why would she no' see the two of them again?" asked Winkie.

"Och weel," said the Brounie, "it is a wee thing sad, thon."

"I'm no' a bairn," said Winkie. "I—I need to know."

"Good and weel," said the Brounie. "Ye shall hear the thing right. The twa brithers were in a kirk in Spain, a

Popish kirk it will have been, and ain o' them gied an orange to a bonny leddy that was at her prayers. But the bonny leddy had a guidman that saw what was passing, and he stickit the yin brither in under the oxter wi' a sharp Spanish knife, and out came the dark heart's bluid, and doun fell the Scottish sodger. But the second brither, he took the Spaniard out frae the kirk and skewert him wi' his bayonet, and a' his friends the same, and this second brither came back to bonnie Scotland and his mither again."

"It is queer", said Winkie, "to think on that happening lang lang syne, and yet I was so near to them. And I canna have the courage to ask you which was the brother that came back to Argyll." He looked round him as though he were trying to get himself right back into his own time again. He said to the piper, "I have lost your sgian on you. The High King gave it a look, and it melted away from me. I couldna' help it."

"If you did no worse than that", said the piper, "you have done well."

"I am asking myself now if the things we were speaking of in yon time came true," Winkie went on. "I canna mind on them in school history. Neilie and the rest, they were aye speaking about votes, and I know sure enough my own father in this time has a vote, but he never bothered his heid about it when it came to the elections. So the voting canna have done much good. But folks arena' put out their houses now. And we live a great way better than then, even with the rationing. And you, Su, you live worse. But there is aye something sore between ourselves and the Big House. I canna scarcely feel it in me this night, not after what we have seen and done together, Su, but back it will come."

"Oh Winkie, what rot," said Su. "It's only you being stupid. And then you get all beastly like your friends at school were to me." For the bruise had come back to her hand, as the shadow had come back to her body.

"They were no friends of mine, yon!" said Winkie fiercely. Su made a mocking face at him.

The piper said, "Well, well, now it is all settled just fine excepting for myself. And since we canna bide behind cold iron all the days of our life, I am asking myself, and I am asking you all, what is to be done now?"

Chapter VII

PHARAOH'S DAUGHTER

———————————— * ————————————

"Has it got to be *now*?" Su said. "I mean—
wouldn't to-morrow morning———"
"And old Morag find him in her kitchen,"
said Winkie. "Nae fears, Su, it just has to be now."

"I don't feel awfully much as if I could save anyone,"
Su said gloomily. She was dreadfully tired; she had ex-
perienced fear and pain; she had said good-bye to delight. It would have been, above all, satisfying to go to
sleep and then to wake up and find none of it had happened. But they were all looking at her, expecting something. She stood on one foot and screwed up her face.
"All right," she said at last. "Can any of you tell me what
I have got to do?"

"You must compel them to give me back," said the
piper, "just the same as you compelled them to give you
back your shadow."

"But I didn't," Su said loyally, "it was Winkie."

"Maybe it will be both of you," the piper said.

"I suppose", Su said slowly, "you really do want to
come back? It was so lovely there. Most of it. You see,
we've both got to come home. There's mother and my
big brothers and—oh the guinea pigs and lots and lots of
things. And Winkie's got all the others at his house."

"Aye, we needed to come home," said Winkie. "But how about yourself? After all, you havena got a home."

Su gave him a jab. It seemed so unkind to say it just like that. But it was as though the piper had been waiting for it. He said, "Aye, but maybe—I have it in my mind that there will be a home for me yet, and that in these very times I am in."

Su said doubtfully, "Do you mean here? I don't know what Morag would say, or Mother. You won't have a ration book, or even an identity card, and what would the policeman say?"

"He can aye say at Lochgilphead he has lost his card, Su," said Winkie hopefully, "and we will give you plenty of herring!"

"But it's not that really," said Su. "It isn't only food and clothes and things that he wants. At least I don't think so. He wants—well, he wants to have a home like everyone else. And he thinks he can have it here. Don't you, Donald?"

The piper said, "It runs in my mind that there is a place for me at the Big House. Aye, in my Father's house there are many mansions. And I have been so long in the Hill."

"The Hill was full of mansions, too," said Su sadly.

"You are not asking me to go back, surely!" cried the piper.

"No," she said. "No, of course not. I only meant—oh, it doesn't matter. Would they do something awful to you if they got you after this?"

"I had a fell fight to win back from them this time," said the piper, "and the next time it might be over hard for me. Did they find you a bonny dance partner, Winkie, my son?"

"Aye," said Winkie, "she was as bonny as—ice cream."

"Cool and soft in the dancing," said the piper softly, "or they might be like the heart of the fire." He turned to the Brounie, "Guardian of the house, what are the bairns to do?"

The Brounie tucked his feet up on to the dresser where he sat as light and canny as a cat among the crockery, "They maun get to their beds afore midnight," he said.

"And I?" asked the piper.

"It is you must unbar the door, *a bhalaich*," said the Brounie.

"My sorrow," said the piper. "Will she know what to do?"

He looked so deep-down sad that Su said quickly, "Don't worry, of course I know. If they change your shape I must hold tight like Tam Lin and Janet. I will shut my eyes."

"I am feared you need to look", the piper said, "just the same as fair Janet did in the story. And as my own wife did, and it was beyond her, the poor thing. And you so young."

"I will help her," said Winkie eagerly. "I dinna care what like things I hold."

"Well," said the piper, "there is no help for it anyway." And he went over to the door and turned the key in the lock, and put it back in the drawer of the kitchen table between Su's blue ration book and old Morag's brown one. Then he lifted his pipes and began to play a lament, and it was terrible heavy on the heart, and the notes of it were forced crying and slow out of the shuddering air, and it was as though there were many voices in it and all sad, and yet none to tell the exact nature of its sadness, nor to know any escape. And through it all Winkie and Su were listening for horse's hooves, and the deliberate steps that would follow.

But the steps were of another kind. They were uneven

and running, and Su had barely time to clutch on to Winkie before the door burst open, and in ran Dugaldina Townsley, with her hair wild and her false-face staring crooked from over her one ear. She went straight for Su without seeing the others. "Miss Susan," she said, gasping. "Ach, Miss Susan, I hae done the most terrible wild *shan* thing on ye!" And then she burst out crying, and the big tears simply popped out of her eyes, and she opened her mouth like a baby.

"What on earth have you gone and done, 'Dina?" said Su. "Oh, do stop it, for goodness' sake!"

"*A Dhia, A Dhia, A Dhia!*" said Dugaldina, and tugged at her hair, that was all over her cheeks and shoulders anyhow. Susan stamped. "Ach, he will come, sure!" said Dugaldina.

Su felt like hitting her, but managed not to. "Who is it, 'Dina?" she said.

"Och, I dinna ken who at all it is, but he isna a right one! He askit me how would he get seeing you, and I thocht—och, I thocht, sure, he was yin of our folk off the road. And I tellt him, Miss Susan, and I wasna' meaning you harm nor skaith, and then I saw, och, he wasna' yin of our folk! He was—he was—ach, I canna like to say who he was!"

"I doubt we know well enough who it was," said Winkie, "and isn't that just like a tink, meddling with what doesna concern ye!"

Dugaldina began to cry furiously again. "Well, I suppose we were kind of expecting him," said Su, "if it was the Prince. I think it must be."

"Aye, the Prince!" sniffled Dugaldina. "The *baro-Rai*! It was himself."

"Go and wash your face, 'Dina, do," said Su. "Look, there's a cloth by the sink." She turned to the piper, "You're sure—you're quite sure, Donald, that you want to meet him? I mean, Winkie could whistle the tune again."

"You canna aye be whistling," said the piper, "and they could get angry, and put their anger on to Winkie. No, it is this way is best. And maybe in the end I will get a home on mortal earth."

And then the Prince of the Fair People came into the kitchen, and Dugaldina sank on to her knees, holding to the corner of the sink, and whispered, "Thon's him!"

"Having been told the way, I am here," said the Prince. And he walked slowly towards them, as a dog walks slowly towards a bird that is going to be shot, and suddenly Su seized hold of the piper's hand. "Well," said the Prince, "is it back with me you are coming, Donul Beg? For the night of Hallowe'en is drawing to its end, and the dance waits for you." And he took from under his cloak a flower of the same kind that Winkie's fairy partner and the other maidens of the Fair People had worn in their hair. There was a faint scent off it, covering the kitchen smell of cocoa and fried herring, and Winkie had a startled look and threw back his head to smell it better.

But the piper moved a little away from it, and towards Su, who didn't really like the smell herself, not entirely. The piper said, "This time it is good-bye, and I am staying, and my home is on mortal earth."

The Prince let fall the flower, and then casually set his foot on it, and they with their eyes fixed on foot and blossom could see the petals writhing and flattening, and hear a tiny heart-breaking scream come up from it. "Oh, you are horrible!" said Su furiously.

The Prince kicked the tattered flower carelessly towards them, and again the piper moved closer to Su, and now she had thrown her arm across him and taken his other hand, but Dugaldina stretched out her fingers timidly and then made a sudden snatch at the flower.

"Look out, 'Dina!" said Su. "It may be magic."

"It's mine's!" said Dugaldina. "The bonny wee floo'er." And then she gave a kind of whimper. "Guid sakes, it's living it is!" For the thing had wriggled round in her hand and turned its hurt petals towards her, like tiny arms. She held it in the hollow of her hands, and her straw-gold hair fell over it as she stared down.

"You know what follows?" said the Prince.

And the piper answered, "I know well."

Then the Prince lifted his hand, and everything began to shake like in an air raid when they are coming close and you are all on the floor waiting for the next one. And like the falling of a bomb something terrible and blinding seemed to happen, and Su was holding in her arms a coiling, wriggling mass of snakes, or one snake, and its head was looking at her, and it opened a fanged earth-smelling mouth.

"Hold it, Su!" cried Winkie. And she managed to see him beyond the snake's body, and to make her hands grip tighter. There was another shuddering, and Su tried desperately to remember the veroos of Tam Lin.

> They'll turn me in your arms, lady,
> An aske but and a snake.

He'd been a snake, oh what was next? The thing in her arms, its body against her own, dissolved and softened and hardened again, and oh, it was a slater, an enormous, frightful slater, with no face, but palps twitching and jaws working and all its grey legs waving in her face!

"Hold!" yelled Winkie, and Su screamed and held and shut her eyes, and felt the thing dissolve again into shuddering.

> They'll turn me in your arms, lady,
> But and a deer sae wild.

Yes! She opened her eyes, and her hands were gripping the rough coat of a wild terrified thing that bounded and leapt, and she couldn't hold it, she couldn't! But Winkie had run in, and was holding it, too, the strong struggling untamed deer. It gave a great swipe down with its horns at them, but Su was below its reach, had her arms round its neck, felt the fierce strength, that was almost too much for her, dissolving again and changing.

> They'll shape me in your arms, lady,
> A hot iron at the fire.

The white-hot thing was so near she could hardly breathe. She must—*must*—get away from it! But her hands weren't burnt—if she didn't look at them—beyond the quivering outline of the white-hot bar, tottering to fall on her, she saw the Brounie on the dresser, who nodded to her. Again she shut her eyes and held.

> They'll shape me in your arms, lady,
> A mother-naked man.

If only they'd finish with it! She felt the blast again, shaking her as the thing changed, and had to look, and there in her arms was a baby, asleep and warm and soft, and not so much as a shawl on him. Somehow Su was so extremely surprised that she almost dropped him. She staggered a little, and felt Dugaldina's hand on her shoulder guiding her to a chair. She sat down with the sleeping baby in her lap, and he seemed to shiver a little. "Oh, he'll catch cold!" she said, and pulled the full skirt of her green party frock up over him.

And then everything was quiet. And the Prince was gone.

Winkie came and stood beside her. He said, "That's him, right enough, Su. But what in all the wide world can we do with a wee baby?"

The baby opened his eyes, which were the same clear

blue as the piper's, but without knowledge or recognition. Yet now he was looking at Su. He was just old enough to smile in an uncertain, delightful way. The smile spread over all his face. He wriggled his arms, not attending to Winkie.

"Oh, isn't he a darling!" said Su, and kissed him.

"You have won him fair, Susan, my hero," said the Brounie, and hopped down from the dresser.

"He'll want some clothes," said Su, looking up, and suddenly feeling worried again. "And I don't suppose he's got a ration book!"

"Och weel," said the Brounie. "We will just tak' a keek in the pot." He trotted up to the Esse stove, hopped on to the top of it by way of the oven door-knob and the bar along the edge, and walked over to the big pot that was keeping warm at the side.

"It's only got soup-bones," said Su, but the Brounie didn't heed. He lifted the lid and grinned. He pulled out a woolly vest and threw it at Su. She sat the baby up and put it on to him. It was delightful getting his fat wavy arms through the sleeves, and the vest was knitted from the softest Shetland wool. One after the other the Brounie threw her all the baby's clothes, warm from the pot, and all of them of the most beautiful material. The flannel petticoat was scalloped and embroidered with white silk. The dress was lawn and lace. The pin for the nappies was surely gold. One shawl was a delicate gossamer of Shetland and the other was cashmere, light and warm and silky, a noble great square. At the very end the Brounie whisked out a blue ration book and an identity card. The name on them both was Donald Ferguson, but in both there was a black blot over the registration number.

"It *is* him," said Su. "Oh Donald, you are a sweetie!" She began to hug him, and he made comic kind of cooing noises, which she appeared to find the greatest fun.

Winkie looked very puzzled. "Do you like him this way, Su?" he asked at last.

"He is my very own," said Su. "At least—do you want to be his father, Winkie?"

"Nae fears!" said Winkie, backing away.

Dugaldina was on her knees beside him. "The bonny wee man," she said. "The *baro chauvie!* Och, see, he gie'd me a wee smile!"

"These lassies is just daft," said Winkie disgustedly to the Brounie, but the Brounie was over looking at the baby, too.

He picked up the baby's hand, and turned it to see the palm and the fingers. "Aye, aye, he willna' ha' lost his giftie wi' the pipes," said the Brounie satisfied.

"Oh," said Su, "isn't that grand. Where shall we send him to school? Do they teach piping anywhere?"

"Time enough," said the Brounie. "He will no' be playing for a wee while, my lassie, but his pipes are here yet, and you will need to keep them safe for him." He pointed, and the children saw the pipes lying in below the kitchen table. Winkie picked them up. He blew softly, and patted the bag as it filled.

"Maybe", said the Brounie, "you could get a lend o' them frae the wee fellow till the time comes on that he is old enough to learn from ye."

"But, are you sure I will be allowed to keep him?" said Su suddenly and anxiously.

"Trust you, ma lassie!" said the Brounie. "And it's myself will be by ye, and that though ye arena seein' me. Ye'll never-ever be feart in days to come when you're by your lane in the Big House?"

"I never was!" said Su indignantly. "Well, hardly. But I just couldn't be now. There, my duckie lamb! His head feels so lovely and wuzzy on my arm. Do feel, Winkie."

Winkie stroked the dark soft hair gingerly. "It is like a wee mole," he said.

"It isn't," said Su crossly. Then she turned to the Brounie. "But is he really the piper? I mean, does he know? Is he somewhere inside?"

"Yon wee bairn is Donald Ferguson," said the Brounie, "but Donald Ferguson doesna ken. He needed to gae back to the Hill, or else to suffer a' things on mortal earth, which is to say death, and a' that goes wi' death. How else did he play his ain lament? But, having suffered, the bairn is in his hame, and in the arms of a lass that loves him, and maybe when the bairn has grown he'll hae an inkling o' things past, and it will come clear in his music, and there is the piper's text fulfilled, lassie of the Big House."

"So it is," she said, "I had clean forgot it. But that was about Moses. He won't be like Moses, will he? Oh, I do hope not!"

"He'll no' make laws, lassie. He'll make music, that is a far and away better thing. And he'll gar folks to dance that had been grieving, and gif he gars them grieve, it will be a glad grieving, and the beginnings o' the thing they have in them to be. And there is the weird I lay on your bairn, Susan, and a good weird it is, and now I will be going my ways, and ye needna mind nae mair on this night's work then ye need to mind." And with that the Brounie gave a hop and a skip and flicked his fingers, and made one spring on to the dresser.

"Oh, mind the plates!" said Su, but as she said it he kicked one of the old soup plates off, and it crashed on to the floor and broke into a dozen bits. "Oh goodness," said Su, "it's sure to wake old Morag!" And somehow or other she was quite sure it would, though she hadn't worried a bit either about the piping or the terrible thunder of the changes. Winkie began hurriedly to pick up the pieces, and Dugaldina began to whimper. "You'd better run, 'Dina," said Su, "and if you try and tell anyone what you saw, they'll think you're bats, and they'll shut you up in the asylum."

"I'll no speak ae word to hurt ye, Miss Susan," said 'Dina, "but I hae the wee floo'er." And she clasped her hands over it where she had put it down the neck of her shirt.

"Throw it away, 'Dina," said Su. "It's magic and it might hurt you awfully."

"Ach no!" said 'Dina, and darted between them as though she thought they were going to take it away from her, and ran through the door and down the steps, and they heard the outer door slamming behind her.

"The silly gowk," said Winkie, "but if she willna be warned——" He began to put the pieces back on the dresser where the Brounie was no longer sitting, but neither of them spoke of that.

"Maybe she will know what to do with it," said Susan. "You see, Winkie—supposing the fairies and the tinkers are related somehow—— Oh, golly, here's Morag coming! But I *will* keep him."

Old Morag had come in haste, with her dressing-gown huddled round her, but without her teeth, so that she was at a certain disadvantage. Her grey hair hung stringily down her back. She began at once to ask what they were doing wakening decent folks from their beds, and it was no use them saying it was Hallowe'en if they couldna behave like Christians. "I'm awfully sorry we broke a plate," said Su, "but it was only one of the old ones."

"I'll be bound he broke it, the deil's bairn that he is," said Morag, mumbling away at Winkie, "and it is a good skelping he should get!" And then she looked at Su, and then she opened the kitchen drawer, and felt in between the ration books, and drew out her spectacles and put

94

them on, and stared, and came nearer and adjusted the spectacles. "What in the name of a' that's guid ha' ye got there?" she demanded.

"Well," said Su, "don't you see what it is?" And she giggled in a way that made Winkie suddenly want to scrag her.

"A wee bairn," said Morag. The baby, who had been in a cat's sleep, opened his blue eyes and smiled at Morag. "Ach, isn't he the bonny wee fellow!" said Morag. "Whatna bairn is he, and what in a' the world is he doing in my kitchen?" She looked round her, blinking, took her spectacles off and put them on again. "Wait you till I get my teeth," she said, mumbling, and scuttled out again.

"I'll get the old cradle out of the attic," said Su, busily planning, "and he can sleep in my room. I know Lizzie's got a bottle that her baby's done with, and I know all about sterilizing them. Winkie, you aren't listening."

"I dinna want to listen," said Winkie angrily, "and ye canna take the baby to the school anyway."

"Morag can look after him while I am at school. She'll like it really, she's always saying she is lonely. He will be able to go to school himself in five years. Oh dear, I hope they have some new paint in the infant room by then! I wonder how soon he can start music. Whistle something to him, Winkie, do, and we'll see if he likes it."

Winkie came closer and bent over the baby. He began to whistle.

"Oh, not that!" said Su suddenly. "Please, not that!"

Winkie stopped. "I must," he said. "I will prove him." And he began to whistle the tinker's tune. Susan had both arms round the baby, her heart was going so hard she thought it would burst out of her, and Winkie whistled, looking at the baby, and the baby dimpled and smiled and

stretched his lips and cooed as though the tune was something nice to eat. Winkie finished it and looked from the
baby to her and nodded.

"Oh," she said, "oh, if it had hurt him, if he'd vanished
or anything, I think I would have died, Winkie!"

"Blethers," said Winkie shortly, "folk dinna die yon
way. But I will teach him to whistle, Su."

Morag came back with her teeth, and her hair pinned
up in a bun. "Did I see right?" she demanded. "I amna
dreaming? Ach no, I couldna dream the like of *him*." And
she glared at Winkie, who pretended not to notice.
"Now", said Morag, "whatna bairn is this?"

"His name", said Su, "is Donald Ferguson."

"Ferguson—Ferguson," said Morag, "there are no Fergusons hereabouts, and havena been this fifty years and
more."

"There is one now," said Su.

"But whose bairn is he?"

"He is mine," said Su, "I found him. He was kind of
given to me, and I am keeping him."

Morag suddenly held out her arms. "Will he come to
me?" She picked him up, and he still smiled. He seemed
to recognize her arms, too, as being a place of security and
comfort. "Ach, the wee lambie, and see the clothes he has
on him. I have never seen the like, never. Not on yourself, even, Susan *m'eudail*. Where got you him?"

"Really, I can't explain," said Su. "Can I, Winkie?"

"It is a great dark secret," said Winkie impressively,
and Morag blinked.

"What will the mistress say?" said Morag.

"She'll say it was quite all right," said Su, "I am sure of
that. Look, he's got his ration book and everything." She
began to finger through the ration book. "Oh look,
they've left him some money. Look, it's pinned in!" She
fingered the heavy Scottish five-pound notes, like blank-

ets. "We'll take him in the bus, shan't we, Morag, and get him some more lovely clothes?"

"That will be just great," said Morag, "but we will get nothing so bonny as he has on, no, not in Glasgow itself, nor yet in London and New York and all. My certie, it is no common bairn this! There, my wee man. Oh, the bonny bright eyes of him! Susan, you are sure that he isna a wee Prince that has been stolen? You didna get him from yon tinks? Well, well, we will see in the papers if that is so."

"I am going to get the old cradle out of the attic," said Su. "Coming, Winkie? I won't be a minute, Morag. Do hold him till I come down."

"Ach yes," said Morag, "you will just bring the cradle down to my own room."

"I will not," said Su, "Donald is *my* baby. Though I don't suppose it matters much where he is so long as he is at home."

She went out with Winkie following, and up the stairs to the attic. There were a whole lot of things piled up there. She looked round at the old engines and the wooden dobbin that she and her brothers had ridden and loved. "This will be fun for him," she said, "and they'll all be played with again. I would love to make him a playhouse like Elspie and I had." Suddenly she saw that Winkie was upset. "What's up?" she said.

"He's mine's too," said Winkie. "He isna to be just the Big House one!"

"I thought you didn't want to be his father, Winkie," she said.

"I dinna want to be his father," said Winkie, "but when I have my own boat I want him to come wi' me."

"But of course he is going to do that," said Su, pulling out an old hip bath and a couple of water-colours in gilt frames, "and so am I. And it's no good saying I'm only a

97

girl, Winkie, because it won't work with me. And after all, what Donald wanted was a home, and he may as well have that twice over. Yes, and he is going to play with the tinkers, and sit next them at the school, Winkie. And you may as well make up your mind to it. Here's the cradle at last. It will want dusting. What on earth is that on top of it? Oh, it's a bit of black-out! It might as well be burnt. Here, give me a hand, Winkie."

Between them they lifted off the black-out, and pulled the cradle out. The old mattress was still in it. Between them they picked up the cradle, and began to carry it down.

Chapter VIII

SU COMES HOME

Su came back from her first term at an English
school aching to be home, and yet feeling it strange.
She got right into the bows of the steamer and
licked the damp air coming at her. But she couldn't speak
about it properly, least of all to her English school friend
who kept asking stupid questions. They weren't stupid
really, but in the mood she was in, Su thought they were,
and didn't answer properly. The English school friend
was called Polly: she wasn't really Su's best friend, but
she was in the same group and her father and mother
hadn't got back properly into their bombed house in
London, so it got decided that she ought to come up for
the first half of the summer holidays with Su. Anyway,
Polly wasn't half bad, only—for one thing, she'd never
been in Scotland before, and kept on getting excited at
the most ordinary things, for instance two awful Paisley
boys in kilts.

Su's big brothers, John and Hugh, had come on ahead;
their school had broken up a few days earlier. Hugh was
batty about fishing now. Su, who liked salmon for dinner,
thought it was silly to make all this fuss and then probably
not catch any, instead of netting them like some of her
friends did. But it didn't do to say that to Hugh. John was

99

working for an Oxford scholarship, and apparently meant not to be interrupted. Anyhow, he didn't come to meet the girls at the boat; Hugh did, but mostly because he wanted to get some more casts.

When they came to the house Su was on the lookout for the pram. She jumped out and ran over and picked up Donald, who was awake. Her own Donald! But horrible Donald looked at her and dropped his lip and simply howled. And she'd only been away three months! Old Morag came out, scolding, and took him out of Su's arms and he held on to her as if *she*—oh well, bother Donald! Su took herself and Polly off to the raspberries, where they buried themselves for a bit.

There were two Port-na-Sgadan girls coming in every morning to help Morag. One of them was a cousin of Winkie's, and Su knew all about her and her boy friends, and could set her off into fits. But this seemed to annoy John and Hugh, who had got awfully respectable and above themselves at their school, and had taken to washing and wearing ties even at home.

Su had explained to Polly that they had adopted a baby, and Polly said she just wished her own mother would do the same. The boys had got used to it in the last two holidays, and poked Donald amiably. Hugh had even made him a toy rabbit. But Su was so upset with his having howled at her that she wouldn't go near him for a whole day. Instead she did all sorts of things she hadn't really intended to do, like getting out the croquet things and having a long game with Polly. Then Polly showed her a cutting-out game, and they got bits of coloured paper all over everywhere. There were two more families of guinea pigs, and it was good fun thinking of names for them. The older guinea pigs remembered Su all right. When Donald didn't!

The grown-ups were coming home in about a week,

but on Saturday a friend of Hugh's turned up. He was called Jim, and he was very polite to Su and Polly; he hadn't any sisters of his own. They went down to the village to get the tail end of his emergency card, and he talked to Su about things out of the newspapers as though she were much older, and of course she played up. There was a gang of boys hanging about by the shop, drinking fizzy orange out of bottles. One of them was Winkie. For a moment he looked to Su just like one of the others, grubby and stupid, and on the whole an enemy. She remembered how she had written him a long letter from her new school in the very first week and another at half term, and he had never answered. But then she thought: what nonsense, it's Winkie! And she went over to the gang, and some of them said "Hullo" or "It's yourself", but Winkie made a face at her and dodged round the corner of the shop. Su talked for a bit to one or two of the others, asked them how school was now, and so on. But she had a sore feel on her, and soon enough she was back with her own lot.

But Winkie had a sore feel, too. He knew fine he had never answered Su's letters, for all he had kept them in his pocket till they were too dirty to read. But what was there he could say? Here she was in the great world, and the things she had seen in London and the south, and now this grand school with flowers and a swimming pool and a gym, and what was he to say? It was no good just to say, "Hope you are well. I am well." No, it wouldna do that. And he had nothing to tell her about that she didna know already. So, although it was aye jagging him to write, he never got round to it. And then she was coming back, and he had the thought of it in his head wild. And yon first day he was over at the house, and he circled round in case she might be out. But she was for ever with the English lassie, or her big brothers with their fine high-class voices that they had now. And he kept in the bushes, and by and bye a pheasant flew out just by him, and he was affronted in case it might be thought he was after the pheasant, and then he said to himself maybe she would come over to the house, and indeed he said as much to his mother, who said it was no' likely, but made some baking all the same. And Su never came. And then on the Saturday with all the folk there—he couldna speak to her.

That way they were both of them unhappy, and Winkie most. But Su and Polly and Jim and Hugh were playing a new card game that Jim had brought with him. And that meant all of them shouting, and they had the wireless turned on as well. In the middle of it the new girl, Winkie's cousin, came in and said, "There's one of the tinks below asking to see you, Susan." "Oh bother," said Su. "Tell her to wait till we've finished this round." But then she forgot all about it, and only remembered when she was going to bed. And anyhow it didn't seem to matter.

She spent the next morning making friends again with Donald, who, after all, had only protested at being rushed. Now he was delighted at having Su and Polly both paying attention to him, and he showed off and was generally rather nice, and when Su sang to him he bobbed up and down and tried to sing too. He couldn't talk yet, but he babbled away as though he knew what it was all about. Su was awfully keen that the others would say he was going to be intelligent.

And then again at tea-time there was the same message. "Oh golly," said Su. "I forgot all about it yesterday. Are they selling baskets, or what, Cathie?"

"What's about it?" said Cathie. "You needn't be running up and down for the tinks. Will I just tell her to go?"

"Oh no," said Su guiltily, and ran down, and there was 'Dina Townsley, with her hair straggling over her thin shoulders, and the queer look of the young tinkers when they know most folk are against them, but have not yet learned to be tough about it. "Oh, hullo, 'Dina," said Su. "I'm awfully sorry I didn't come yesterday. I didn't know it was you. Where are you stopping now?"

"Over by the tree, Miss Susan," said 'Dina, and her eyes shifted from Su to Polly and Jim who had come down behind her.

"And how's everyone?" Su went on.

"We are fine," said 'Dina, and then, in a kind of whisper, "*Bing*, Susan, *bing* here!"

Su knew a little of the tinkers' language, and she was quite sure 'Dina wouldn't use it to her for nothing, so she said to the other two, "I'll be back in a minute," and slipped off round the wood-shed to 'Dina. Then she said, "What is it?"

'Dina looked all round her, and at last she whispered, "I hae a warning for ye, Miss Susan dear."

"A warning?" asked Su stupidly.

"Aye," said 'Dina. "It is They Yins. They're after the *chauvie*—the wee fellow."

"Donald? But——" And it suddenly came to Su that she no longer believed much in what had or might have happened last Hallowe'en. That had all gone back into a kind of dream. Nothing was left except Donald. And she had made an explanation about Donald, and it had all been accepted. And so had become true. It had been accepted because of the war coming to an end, and Christmas, and Mother's somehow wanting someone else to look after—and—and perhaps the Brounie, and by now she half believed that Donald had just been left with them one night. She shook her head. "They aren't real, 'Dina."

"Are they no'? *Deek!* It was she that gie'd me the warning." And out from the front of her dress 'Dina took the fairy flower, and it was the very same flower that the

Prince had thrown down in the kitchen, and the smell of it was the same disturbing smell. "Ach, Miss Susan, Miss Susan dear, ye should ha' listened yon first time! They could ha' been at him by now."

"We'll see," said Su briefly. "Come on, 'Dina."

In the afternoon Donald was usually in his play-pen on the lawn at the side of the house. Yes, there he was, in pink overalls, holding himself up against the side, having as usual pushed everything he wanted through the bars. "Well, that's all right," Su was saying, when they saw a squirrel bounce out of the play-pen holding something in its teeth, and streak across the lawn, a red-gold feather, and off into the trees. "What on earth! . . ." said Su.

But 'Dina was trembling. "*A Dhia, A Dhia*, it is Him! And that in his teeth, that was the wee one's soul!" And then she burst into tears and ran.

Su had made one rush at the play-pen and knelt beside Donald and stared at him. He was still holding on to the bars, and then something awful happened. Out of the baby's mouth, which was so soft and bright, came a small adult voice, the voice of a little old man, and it said, "Away wi' you, I hate you." And out of the baby's blue eyes came a look of hatred and knowledge. Su gave one yell, and old Morag came flying out.

"There something wrong with Donald!" she gasped. "Oh Morag," she said—but somehow she couldn't repeat it. Morag gave her a look, and said, "It's yourself that has something wrong, surely, Susan *m'eudail*. Come away in out of the sun, now." And before she knew where she was, Su had a thermometer in her mouth, and a horrible cloth wrung out of vinegar plastered firmly on her forehead.

When it was clear she hadn't a temperature, Morag said she could sit out on the lawn in the shade, but not to go racing round now. So there she sat, looking at the baby and he at her, but oh, not—not he himself! And she couldn't read, and she didn't want to play anything. When Morag took Donald off to his bath and supper, she went too and hung over them, and Morag was quite cross and said how could she be so silly, and the wee man doing just grand. "Can I just say good night to him?" Su said, and while Morag was emptying the bath, she leant over his cot, and perhaps it would be all right, she thought, it was only something she had imagined. But again that dreadful little voice said: "Off wi' you, now, you sneaking mawsie! You'll spoil my sport." It was too much. When Morag came back she was in miserable tears, and the next thing she was put to bed with an aspirin and the curtains drawn.

She went to sleep. And then she woke up. And the house was quite still. And after a bit she heard the clock strike, and it was two in the morning. She opened her door a little and listened. Did she or didn't she hear footsteps? If she screamed now Polly would hear, wouldn't she, or one of the boys, but what could she say to them? If only Winkie was here.

She went on tiptoe up the next flight, and looked towards the door of the wee room where Donald was sleeping, in what used to be her own cot. There was a crack of light under the door. She took a step nearer along the passage. It was a yellow narrow light, but between herself and it was a square of white moonlight from the window. That window that used to be such a job to black out. Did she or didn't she hear voices? A dog growling? And could it—oh could it—be the beautiful hound with the golden collar?

She shivered and waited, rubbing one bare foot on the other, pushing back her plaits over the collar of her blue pyjama jacket. If she screamed now Morag would hear. And it would be even less possible to explain.

Then the Brounie was in the silver square of moonlight, his finger on his lips. She could have hugged him.
He came to her. "Sae ye ken?" he whispered. Su nodded.
"It's no' just canny to be standing here", he said, "wi'
their Noble Selves in by. Come your ways noo, lassie."
He took her hand, and pulled her towards him, down to
his own height, to lower yet, below the level of the
window ledge. All the walls of the passage were towering
up! And just at her hand a kind of ragged dark archway.
He pulled her in after him, they were in a cave. The
Brounie had the cheery wee green light in his hand; he
pulled Su on again for a few steps between great rocks.
"Where are we?" she asked.

"In at the back o' the wall," he answered. "But we
needed to go wee, the two of us. We're safe enough, but
listen now!"

Behind them and high up they could hear the boom of
immense voices, which, because of their largeness, were
not intelligible. There were footfalls that shook down
dust all round them, and then, nearer yet, a great terrible
snuffling sound, as though the air all round them were
being sucked in and then blown back, with a strong smell
of dog in it. "Aye," whispered the Brounie, "he's winded
us, but it's as weel he canna speak on't or his masters
would ken. We are couthie and bien here." The enormous
noises had gone by, and the Brounie reached out his hand,
and there was a mouse almost as tall as Su, with great
whiskers like ropes. It looked at them without interest,
and went on its business.

"What happened?" Su whispered anxiously.

"Och well," said the Brounie, "it is this way. They are
angered that Donald Ferguson was ta'en frae them, and
they are on to revenge theirsel's on the lassie that did the
thing. So they hae done the same thing that they hae
done times without mind. They hae ta'en the cradle bairn

and left a changeling in his place. Ye should ha' heeded the first warning."

"I know," said Su guiltily, and sniffed. "Oh please, what will they do with him?"

"They willna want to harm him ava. They will want to foster him up theirsel's, but to do hurt and skaith to you and your house by leaving a piece o' their ain black wickedness under yon bairnie's skin. And gin things are left the way they are, it's sore and sorry ye're like to be when the bairn is a man grown."

"Oh gosh," said Su. "What am I to do?"

"There was a thing folks did in the old bygane days," said the Brounie. "They would take the cradle bairn that was changed and let on they would throw him in the fire, and at the last, when the flames were touching him, in came Themsel's to snatch away their ain and bring back the ither. But, would you hae it in you to hold the wee fellow to the flames, Susan?"

Su shuddered. "Isn't there any way else?"

"Aye," said the Brounie, "you may gang and seek the bairnie at their ain hands, and win him back frae them."

She didn't answer for a minute. She only wanted the whole thing not to have happened. Not just at the beginning of the holidays, anyway, with everything looking like loads of fun. But it had happened. Suddenly she said, "What about Winkie?"

"Better it would ha' been", said the Brounie, "if him and yoursel' had been together, the pair o' ye, but the way things ha' fallen oot it just canna be, unless he was to seek you, my lassie. But that could be."

"Could it?" said Su doubtfully. "Well—it wasn't my fault, anyway. But would I have to go back into the past like I went before?"

"As wee as ye are?" said the Brounie. "Na, na, and I canna work on time and on measure baith at the yince."

He scratched his head. "Ach, I hae it. If ye gang yon gait just yourself and no' your body, then there is naething to it though you are muckle or wee."

"But I can't go without a body," said Su. "Oh please, it was bad enough without a shadow!" And she jumped about with anxiety.

"Dinna be daft," said the Brounie impatiently. "You can take whatna body ye've a mind to. You could be the high queen o' the eagles, Susan."

"Could I fly?"

"Aye, aye, bird shape or beast shape can ye be, my lassie, till the thing is done in time that will work on measure."

"I don't know what you mean."

"I dinna rightly ken mysel'," said the Brounie, "and me as as wee as a wee mousikie! But what is borne in upon me to say is what I am needing to say, and gif ye start on the right path ye'll find the thing ye're seeking. It is the queerest thing, Susan *m'eudail*, but the good is aye stronger than the bad, though whiles it doesna seem so at the first."

"Well," said Susan, "I don't really know what you're talking about, but I suppose I had better get on to the right path and get it over." She looked round, but there didn't seem to be any kind of path at all. Only the foot-printed dark tunnels of the giant mice.

"Mak' your choice then," said the Brounie, and then, "Come away now, what'll ye be?"

"Can it be any kind of beast?" said Su doubtfully.

"A' that is *inter regalia*," said the Brounie. "That is, the King's beasties. Och, lassie, lassie, where's your schooling? The deer, the swan, the eagle, the unicorn, the salmon and the sturgeon, the lion——"

"I'll think I'll be a lion!" said Su. "No, I won't, I'll be an eagle! No, I'll be a swan!" She jumped up and down, but the Brounie was writing marks on the thick plaster-dust. He made a square with a cross inside it. The cross had lines through it that ended in loops. He broke the lines of the cross here and there, rubbing them out with his thumb, joining the broken lines to one another, so that they made a continuous line. You had to look very quickly to see how it was going, moving your eyes, skimming along the lines, no, that wasn't quick enough, running, flying——

Chapter IX

BEING A SWAN

----•----

The great white swan was circling over Port-na-Sgadan. The storm winds coming over the hills lifted her as waves lift a well-built boat. Throat and wings stretched and quivering, she circled up and up. In the joy of it time passed, whether back or forward. Circling down on a lulling after-wind, the swan observed Port-na-Sgadan and the landward parts for many miles beyond.

But she found it a wee bit puzzling. Where was the road? It seemed to go a different way, right up the glen where the old ruins were. But they weren't ruins, they were steadings, with cornery oat fields between the rocks, clachans, with children and cattle going in and out, the bright flying hair of lassies running, the flash of a bucket at the spring, a colt throwing his heels up! Down she came to look nearer at the folk, the air vibrating against the stiff feathers of her wings. Out of the black houses with their low doorways the people of the clachan came running, wives catching their shawls about their heads, crying at their bairns to come ben. The thick human smell of the houses, peat smoke and dung, rose into the swan's nostrils. She circled low enough to see a woman throw up her hands and scream, and the wheel she was spinning at over-set and the basket of wool rolling on the ground. Now men and lads came hurrying in from the fields, waving sticks and shouting, with their short ragged kilts that matched the tartan on the women's heads and shoulders. There was a white splash of spilled milk on the ground and a wee boy fallen over a stone, bare legs and dowp. And all at once it came to the swan that she herself was the cause of all this stramash below on the ground. And with a tilting of her flight feathers she levelled off and then mounted again, away down the glen and back over the Big House.

She circled round, wondering when she was. She couldn't see what had happened to the house, till suddenly she realized that the west wing just wasn't there at all. So it must be before—last time. Before Elspie and Phemie and the play-house. There were some gentlemen by the front steps of the house, all on horseback, and two ghillies in kilts holding the horses. The riders had lovely bright-coloured coats, tartan or deep blue or red, with gold lace on them, and laced hats and swords and shiny boots. She had to look closer. She came swooping down, and the horses plunged and one broke away and bolted, throwing rider and ghillie. The man on the ground scrambled up and seized hold of a gun from a young lad that was holding them, and began to load it in what seemed an awfully complicated way, and suddenly it was pointing at the swan, and bang it went and blue smoke coming, and the swan gave a kind of flapping jump in the air, but the balls had missed by a good yard. She heard one of the gentlemen crying to the one that had shot that he mustna' do sic a thing, to shoot at a swan, it was the maist terrible bad luck it would bring! But the swan was off and away and up into the high clouds again.

Up there the swan played among bull's-eye rainbows in cotton-wool land, or above acres of endless silver.

Strands of time passing were tangled and lost here. Once more she came through, but there were houses on fire and people fighting. She couldn't make out what it was all about, or which was the right side, and she didn't like to go near, because they kept on shooting arrows. Besides, there were several eagles about, and they might be going to eat the dead people—or her. They had bright unkind eyes like stones.

She went back up into the clouds and winds again, yet at last she dived, beak forward, stream lining her wing and tail feathers, the cold bright air rippling through her down. She was up on the ridge of the hills now, and as she came closer she could see deer running among the heather and hardly any sheep. There were more woods, too, thick tangly kind of woods that might have had anything living in them. It was nice to go planing over, her body stretched out behind her long neck.

There seemed to be rather less cultivation now, though the clachans of the clansmen were still strung along the glen. She came down on to the loop in the river near where the house should be. There was no garden at all, no road, and the Big House that was so rambly with all the bits different people had built on to it, it had gone into a sort of hard little square tower with a few huts and byres round it. Somehow the swan didn't like that. She felt lonely. She wanted to stop flying and come down to earth or water. She flew low over some more dark woods, the thick rounded tops of oak, and some Scots pine, but no larch nor spruce. And then there was a break and in a clearing a mixed herd of cows, horses, goats and sheep, a patch of some kind of crop, two or three big fires and a whole lot of folk doing all sorts of things.

As she came nearer the problem of landing troubled her, but at the join of the burns was a lochan, shallow with summer, reeded round, starry here and there with water-

lilies, cool and welcoming for a Su or a swan. She came
down into the wind, and the blue face of the water tilted
and rose at her, was suddenly near. Her under-body hit it,
bounced, slipped, she braked with wings and tail, scut-
tered along, recovered herself among lily-pads and spread
her great foot-webs to walk deliciously on buoyant
water.

The white water-lily flowers, tinted on their outer
petals with green and watery rose, had golden centres,
attractive to dragonflies. There were small fairies in a few
of them, who pulled the petals over their heads as the
great swan sailed by, her neck arching high above them.
At the edge of the lochan, in a gap between the reeds,
there was a young lassie sitting on a fallen tree, with her
bare toes in the mud, working on a willow basket. A
little way further along the bank, under an oak tree,
there were some men with hide aprons all down their
fronts hammering away at something. The sound of tapping on metal came jumping out and sometimes a small
shower of sparks. They seemed, some way, separate from
the rest of the folk that the swan could see beyond the
lassie and to the other side, whenever she stretched up her
long neck. That way there seemed to be men and boys
skinning a deer. They were wearing long plaids, over
their left shoulders, and then belted, so that the ends were
pleated into a kind of kilt. Some of them had bits of deerskin round their legs. Beyond them again were low
houses built of stones and turf, with turf or heather roofs,
and a few kind of tents made of deerskins. The swan was
wondering when at all it could be.

She paddled nearer to the lassie on the bank, who was
wearing a sort of shapeless woven shirt of green and
brown, pinned at the shoulders, and with a belt of
plaited rushes. She had yellow hair hanging over her thin
shoulders, just like—why, it was 'Dina.

Being a Swan

The lassie lifted her head and stared at the swan. The swan, embarrassed, tucked up one foot under her wing and pretended to preen the feathers over it with her beak. At last the lassie spoke. She was, naturally, speaking in the Gaelic: what else? But that was no difficulty at all. It was like the way you can be hearing a song, both the tune, which is one thing, and the words, which are quite another, and yet coming out of the one mouth and going into the one pair of ears. Just the same for Su in her swan shape, she could hear both the Gaelic that was spoken and the meaning of what was said. And it appeared to be the same for those listening to herself. For there was always a slight puzzlement on them, and yet they always understood her. The lassie said, "How at all are you here?"

Su said, "I am looking for you know who. Are they here?" The lassie didn't answer at all. She looked sidelong, and suddenly picked up her basket and began a quick weaving in and out of the split willows. What she was making was a tall basket with a pattern of red squares on white. A woman went by between her and the men, with a baby on her back in the neuk of the plaid, the same way 'Dina's mother used to carry her youngest, wee Rachel. At last she asked again, "It is yourself, 'Dina, isn't it?"

The lassie said, very low, "Aye, it's me. But it is not me myself, not how you were thinking."

"Well, anyway, can you tell me when it is?" asked the swan.

"When?" said the 'Dina lassie. "It is now."

"Yes, but——" The Su swan scratched her head, which she could do easily with the foot which was out of water. "But what King is there, what King in Edinburgh?"

"Och yes, they say there is a King there right enough," said the lassie, "but he does not bother his head with us, nor we with him, and the Lord of the Isles is far enough.

But there is the Chief here that is a young lad still, the way his father was killed."

This didn't seem to help at all. Except that there was a King in Edinburgh, and there was a Lord of the Isles. So perhaps it was somewhere in that rather muddling time that was called the Dark Ages in the history books, before you got to William Wallace or Mary Queen of Scots or anyone you could be really interested in. She thought she had better try something else. She said, "'Dina, are— Those Ones—about at all?"

"Aye," said 'Dina, "they are never far."

"Have they got Donald?"

"Which Donald?"

"My Donald. You know. Have they got a baby?"

"They are aye taking the babies. They are aye putting their power on to folk for ill, or whiles for good. Yes, and on to the kye and the sheep and the horses and the houses even. But when we are going to the church we have a bigger power and a stronger sign." She crossed herself quickly, and then her hand went to the neck of her dress, and she pulled out a flower, and it was the same flower. She held it to her ear, bending her head over, and then spoke quickly. "She says—she says the ones you are seeking are near at hand, and the babe is safe, but she says there is danger to you—danger from the Big House."

"From *my* house?" said swan Susan indignantly.

"Maybe it is not your house now," said the lassie. From beyond them rose a shout. The men who were skinning the deer had jumped up, and one of them was waving a big knife. Men and women hurried out of the huts, and then several people came riding out of the wood on small, rough horses with gilt and coloured leather harness, and they themselves—five men and a boy it seemed to be— had tartan plaids, and some of them were wearing chain armour. The swan was stretching her neck, to see better, was wading up on to the soft mud of the bank, but suddenly the 'Dina lassie spoke. "Danger," she said, "danger from them! You must fly."

"But why?" asked swan Susan. "Perhaps they could tell me——"

"They will not!" said 'Dina, and then, very quickly, as the riders turned their way, "Go! *Bing avri!*" And somehow it made the thing suddenly serious that it should be in the tinkers' language, the warning to go, and the swan pushed off through the reeds and went faster and faster, paddling and flapping, and at last got clear of the water, airborne again, circling and wondering.

She made another wide flight over the forest, seeing the patches of cultivation round the clachans, the small flocks and herds guarded by half-bare children, or girls carrying their distaffs and spinning. If she came down low the beasts would take fright and bolt, which was sometimes rather fun. There were a few boats out with their sails set, but none very far from land. It looked as if they were fishing with very small nets.

The place was dotted with lochans and swamps, far more than there were in Su's real time, but perhaps, she thought, they have been drained, or rather they're going to be. Anyway, they were nice places for swans. Some of them had swans on them already, and Su thought it would be fun to make friends. But the other swans didn't seem to think so at all. They stuck out their necks and hissed, and the things they were saying were the same things that nasty little boys and girls say when a stranger comes into the school. So the Su swan, who was just going to come slipping down among them, beat hard on the air, and before going on bent her neck straight down and hissed a remark at them which was quite as rude as theirs. Some of them would have liked to chase her, but it took them far too long to get under way, and, being swans, they couldn't throw stones.

She sailed off again, and then saw another lochan, an even nicer one with a wee rocky island and spikes of arrowhead and blue bogbean flowers round the edge. Nobody had ever cut rushes or willows here. Nobody had ever fished for the trout which ringed the smooth water with rises or skimmed below the Su swan's paddling toes.

And then between the tall rushes she saw the riders again. Two of them had dismounted and were coming slowly towards the loch. The boy was in front. He was holding a bow almost as tall as himself in his left hand. He stood very still, and one of the men put an arrow into his right hand, and he drew back the string of the bow and still the Su swan paddled in to the bank, wondering what he was going to shoot at, and suddenly saw he was aiming straight at her, and also saw that he was Winkie. With the arrow drawn back to its head, she yelled at him, and her hand—her wing—chucked up to shield her face. But the loosed bowstring had shot the arrow, and oh, oh, it was sticking in her arm—her wing—no, it *was* her arm, her very own right arm, and this awful arrow clean through it, and as she looked the blood began to run right down to her elbow, and she felt awfully sick and fell on her knees in the shallow water, calling, crying, for Winkie.

Chapter X

WINKIE'S CASTLE

They were picking her up. She felt something being wrapped round her, but everything was swimming and her eyes were screwed up with pain and fright. And then something awful seemed to be happening to her hurt arm. And Winkie was saying, "Stick it, Su, please stick it! Su, my darling, I didna ken it was you. Ach, Su——" And then suddenly it wasn't quite so bad, and she half opened her eyes and saw Winkie's face with the tears rolling down it, and he seemed to be wearing a kind of small crown. And then she looked down at her own arm, very gingerly, and the arrow was out of it—they must have broken its head off—and one of the men was tying it up. She looked away, back at Winkie. He said, "I didna ken it was you, Su, till you cried out, and it was too late; and I could have died. Su, oh Su, is it hurting terrible?" She nodded, but already she knew it was hurting less. She was lying on the grass wrapped in a plaid, and it occurred to her that when she had taken her own shape she probably wasn't wearing any clothes at all. Well, it didn't matter anyway. They were all being nice to her, and Winkie was back. They picked her up, and one of the men carried her in front of him on his horse. She leant back, watching through half-shut eyes, tree-tops and sky and the man's grave face and his curly brown beard. Another man was carrying something white on his arm; yes, it was her feathers, her swan dress. Sometimes Winkie rode beside them, and he kept on asking was she all right, and she said yes, but now her arm was throbbing a good deal.

She had shut her eyes for a bittie and wasn't thinking of anything but the arm, when the jogging of the horse stopped and there were more voices, and she saw they had come to the little castle that she had seen in the same place where the Big House was to be later. She was carried in and put on a kind of bed of feather pillows, with lovely soft otter and beaver skins over them. It was rather dark, and smelt like the inside of a cottage, heavy with peat smoke and food and people and dogs. There were several women helping her. They put her on a long kind of linen shirt, and washed her face and her hand, which was all sticky with blood. The warm water smelled of roses. She was thirsty. They brought her some not very nice milk, and then a drink that reminded her a little of whisky, but instead of having a nasty taste, it had a lovely taste of heather honey. She lay blinking at the women with their heavy, rather shapeless, dresses of linen or wool with long sleeves and fringed mantles pinned at the shoulders with brooches, and all with stiff white handkerchiefs over their hair. They put a cool fold of linen under her head, and a linen sheet over her. And then Winkie was back, looking awfully worried, and he seemed to have very fine clothes with a lot of gold on them and a great necklace, and there was a nice oldish man with him, wearing what looked like a white nightgown, and clean shaven. He came up to her and sprinkled her with water out of a silver cup, and said something in Latin, and watched her, so she smiled at him because he had a nice face. And then he lifted his hands and spoke again in Latin that had a soothing hum-

ming sound, and she went to sleep. When she woke up it
was much darker. There were torches in the square hall
and a smell of smoke and resin. Winkie was sitting beside
her. She began at once. "Why did he sprinkle water on
me, Winkie?"

"He is the priest," said Winkie. "It is holy water yon,
and if you had been of evil it would have burned you. I
was telling him you were entirely of good, Su, but he
needed to try you, and when he saw it was so he gave
you a God's blessing, and while you were asleep he put
ointment and bandages on your arm, and he says it is
healing well. Ach, Su, it seems I am to be aye and always
hurting you."

"I can't think why on earth you wanted to shoot me,
Winkie. Who are you now, anyway?"

"I am the Chief here, and it was laid on me to shoot the
lone swan, but I never knew it was you."

"How have you managed to be Chief?"

"Ach, well, my father was killed, and the rest thought
I had the makings of the thing in me, but I have needed to
take on the blood feud, Su."

"Well, but how did you come here anyway? The last
time I saw you, Winkie, you were sucking fizzy lemonade out of a bottle behind the shop, with—with all your
real friends!"

"Do you think that, Su? Do you think it truly? And
me following you back through the long years of the
past."

"Well, you'd better tell me what happened. I say,
Winkie, is there anything to eat?"

"My soul, all that is mine is yours." He had spoken
then in the Gaelic. Sometimes he was doing that and
sometimes speaking in his old way. It was as though he
were not very certain which of two people he was, or
wanted to be. Now he called over his shoulder for food of

the best, and his people came running. He *is* the Chief, she thought. They brought oatcakes and honey and thick cream and crowdie, all on a big wooden plate with carving round the edge, and someone else brought delicious wild raspberries. It was all a bit messy, but she ate bits of everything, and when she was finished they brought a bowl of warm rose-smelling water to wash her hand. And while she ate Winkie explained everything that had happened. "The Brounie came for me," he said, "and told me how things had gone with yourself, and at the very first I said 'Ach, to hell', for the way it was, I was terrible sore at you."

"At me? Why on earth? . . . *You* never answered my letter, you pig, Winkie!"

"Well, it isna worth speaking on now, for it's all past. But syne I said I must seek my lassie, and I would go to wherever in the past you were, and then the two of us together we would find the wee fellow, and all would be well. And then the Brounie made a mark on the floor of the wee room off the kitchen where I slept in that time, and he said whenever I was to see yon mark I was to lay my hand on it, and it would take me to yourself. So the next place I was, my folk had a wee croft up the glen, and we were far enough from the Big House, and it was kind of cheery in the clachan with all the folk knowing one another, and the head ones saying how the cropping and grazing were to go. For we didna each have a field, but the corn was grown in rigs in each of the corn-fields, and a rig to each household. I mind on that and standing by the heads of the rigs and thinking to myself it was poor stuff, mostly bere, but yet folk were gey glad of it and speaking comfortably of the year that was passed and the year to come. And then, Su, then there was a great screeching and flyting behind me among the houses, and when I turned there was a muckle great swan coming down like a bomber, and it must have been yourself, though I didna know it."

"Did you ever find out when that was, Winkie?"

"Ach, it will have been three seventies of years back from the time we were used to, for there were folk that were speaking of the Stewarts, and maybe things would be better with them back in the stead of yon English kings in London, but most of us didna heed on that."

"Why does it go in seventies, Winkie?"

"Ach, I dinna know. One canna aye be asking questions—not without one is a lassie! So in a while I was drawing water from the spring, and I saw below me through the water yon same mark on a stone at the bottom. So I was wraxing down to lay my hand on it, and it was deeper than I thought, and I fell, ach, I fell through the spring water. But that wasna the whole of it. I fell through times of the world, with my hand aye out towards yon mark, and all about me was darkness and a kind of humming, and I wanted terrible to get my hand on it, and at last my fingers seemed to touch it, and syne I had my hand on it right and grasping it, but by then it wasna the mark on any stone, it was the hilt of a sword, Su, and my own sword at that. And what I was doing was this, I was pulling at yon sword with my two hands, for the thing was stuck—— Ach, I dinna like to tell you!"

"Do go on, Winkie. I believe I can guess."

"Well then, Su, it was stuck between a man's ribs, just the same as it could have been a rotten tree, and I had killed the man." Su gasped and flushed, and a new pain seemed to go through her bandaged arm, and yet some way she liked the serious look that Winkie had. She took his hand. It was Winkie's hand, right enough, and queer, it shouldn't be inky, nor sticky with herring scales. He had a silver ring on one finger, with a beautiful fine pattern of black enamel on it. He went on. "I knew I had the greatest need of yon sword to kill other men and to defend myself, and I stuck my heel on the man's dead face and pulled my sword free, but it wasna clear to me who I was fighting, nor why. I only knew that they had come on us, and we hated them, Su. I had it in me to use my sword well, and before the fighting was over I had killed another man."

"When would that have been, Winkie? Do you know at all? Could it have been Wallace or Bruce or anyone out of history?"

"I dinna ken. Only, when we were shouting at our enemies or abusing the prisoners we took, we would call them English. English cowards—Dirty Edwards. Aye, and my folk had two-three English slaves."

"Slaves?"

"Ach, well, they would have been prisoners from some other war that hadna been ransomed. We werena bad to them. It was just that they had the slave rings on their necks, and they did the most of the heavy work. But all the same they were mostly like ourselves. They ate the same food, and they had learnt to speak right."

"The Gaelic?"

"What else? Yet we had some words of French, Su, and—and maybe Norse. I mind on one of my uncles speaking of Norroway, and of some cattle and gear he had in a town there."

"Winkie——" She hesitated, then came out with it. "You have come up in the world, haven't you? I mean, it sounds as if your folk were some of the head ones."

"That will have been so, I am thinking. But, after all, it would be a queer world if the same ones were aye up or aye down. It isna that way that things go, and if it were there would be nothing to keep us from the terrible great sin of pride. It could be, Su, that in such times my folks were big and your folks were wee. Or that they were the same. But I didna think on't, for there was this fighting that went on for two-three days, and in the evenings it would mostly stop, and we ate till we couldna take another bite, and there was singing, aye and playing on pipes and harp. I liked it fine. And minding on what I had done, and thinking on what I was to do the next day. And that next day came with more fighting, and the wolves coming down from the hills and howling and yowling to eat the folk that were killed. And the eagles after the same. And, Su, there was one swan. Was that yourself?"

"I did see some fighting, Winkie. I wish I'd known you were there. I would have come down."

"Better you hadn't," said Winkie, "because—ach, well, Su, I am thinking I got myself killed the second day after the swan came. But it didna hurt me any. And maybe it wasna that, but we were fighting close, and I was wild angry and keen, and kind of mad the way things werena going the way my lot wanted. And I saw yon mark on the breast of a man, and I let my shield arm drop, and I reached for it, aye, with my whole body some way, and—and he would have got me sure on that. It is like football, and if you dinna pass when you should, then you are done. And I mind of the same headlong falling and darkness, and at the last I was close to the mark, but it seemed all blurred by my own sadness, and it was on the cover of a book. Aye, of the Gospels. And I was taking an oath upon it, and yon one that you saw with the holy water, he was holding it out to me. And the sadness was on me because I had seen my father dead with a spear clean through him."

"Oh, Winkie, I'm sorry! Was it the priest who was holding the book? Does he live here?"

"Aye, he is the priest of the castle. He was terrible kind

to me after my father was killed and the rest making me do the tests. He put me under all kinds of protection."

"What from? I don't understand."

"Ach, well, maybe ghosts and that. Or yon same ones we have had our dealings with before now. They could have been at me the same way that they could have been at the cradle bairn, and me not yet the Chief. But I am that now. And I have found you, Su, and you are under my protection and my roof, and you will have praise and honour from my folk."

"Is this really your castle, Winkie, where the Big House was?—I mean, where it's going to be?"

"It is on me the safety and greatness of the castle is at this time."

"It isn't awfully great," said Su, looking round. "It's just one big square room, and I suppose another one on top, and those funny little stone steps in the corner—oh Winkie, don't look so cross! It's a very nice castle." She was half frightened the way Winkie had looked at her for a moment.

He said, in the Gaelic, "There are those that think otherwise."

"Yes, of course," she said, "it is only that I haven't got used to it. I mean sleeping and eating and everything in one room. Though it is a big room. And it makes it more kind of private being so dark. But, of course, the torches are lovely, Winkie, only one couldn't read by them."

"Who would want to read", said Winkie, "when there is singing and story-telling? Listen!" He held up his hand. Someone was playing on a harp, queer ripply kind of music, and then half singing and half talking, but with a sort of chorus that everyone joined in. "They will put into the song about the swan-maid, Su, yourself. You will be for ever living in yon song. They will make you a clothing of words that are as beautiful as the far great hills of Morvern on a clear day." And it was the queerest thing, thought Winkie, how I should have said yon, and I have never seen Morvern, and yet and yet. . . . But this one, whose shape I have taken, he has seen Morvern, has hunted there with the Chiefs, learnt to shoot with the bow as I can shoot now. He looked down at Su lying on the pillows, and again a pain went through him, thinking how near he had been to being her death. He must tell her how it had all happened—now, at once. In the half dark he looked at her closer. She seemed gey tired and white-looking, and it was his doing.

"Su," he said, "can you listen a wee whilie more? I had been over to the bay to settle a quarrel about a boat, and there was a tall and noble-looking woman in a green mantle standing by the side of the path. She said she had a warning for me, that when I saw a swan flying or swimming alone I must shoot it, and this on peril of my life. Now a swan is a half royal bird, but myself being the Chief I could do the thing. I was wanting to ask more, and so were those with me, but the woman having given the warning had gone on. We cried on her to stop, but she wouldna, so we followed her, and soon the horses were going beyond the walk, and there was no sign of a hurry on the green-mantled woman, and her feet never lifted to run, but try as we might our horses could never gain on her, and in a while she was not there at all. So we talked and we better talked, and in the end it was thought by all that I must take the warning or ill would come of it, and there is how I came to shoot you, Susan."

"I see. I suppose she was one of—Those Ones?"

"Aye. She knew well enough who was the swan. But, Su, she said one other thing. She would come back after seven days, and see had I done what it was laid on me to do. And if she comes back——"

"Oh, don't speak to her, Winkie! She might be angry

and hurt you." Su was almost whimpering. She was tired, and her arm hurting again, and she was lost in the past, without Mother or old Morag or anyone to tell her the arm would be all right soon, and kiss her good night. Nobody except Winkie. And Winkie was changed. He had a sort of burning hard look, and he said, "I might get powers against her and the rest of them. I will speak to the priest."

"But you couldn't tell the priest about—us, Winkie?"

"About Su from the Big House, and Winkie from the village, is it? Nae fears! But about the Chief and the swan-maiden, surely. And that is what we are, the two of us."

"I see," said Su, and chewed an end of her own hair, meditating on how to deal with this. She supposed it was all right. The whole thing wasn't taking any of time in the twentieth century. It wouldn't really have mattered if she had been shot dead. Or—would it? Everything seemed awfully real. She had even caught a flea. There were so many dogs snuffling about in the rushes on the stone floor, and most of them looked as if they had fleas. At last she said: "Anyhow, Winkie, what we are here for is to find Donald."

"Aye," said Winkie. "Aye, that is so. I was forgetting."

Chapter XI

WINKIE'S PRISONER

———————— * ————————

The sunlight came shafting into the hall through the narrow windows, showing up a kind of ordered muddle of things, piled-up weapons of war and hunting, an iron plough-soc and a sowing basket, and people sitting on the floor or on benches doing one thing or another, making or mending, and moving among them the gold circle on Winkie's head, giving him protection. In the room below, which was kitchen and store, there would be grain and meal sacks, a quern for grinding, and wooden tubs of butter and salted meat, and in the women's room above there was a loom and stuff half woven, baskets of different coloured wools, jars of dye-stuffs and the precious embroidery threads. There were a few chests for storing things, but no cupboards and no comfortable chairs.

The sunlight shifted from rush to rush on the floor. Every few weeks the rushes would be thrown out into the midden, just the same as litter from the byres. Meanwhile, they gathered bones and the leavings of porridge and every other kind of mess. Winkie shuffled his feet in the rushes and looked across to where Su was still asleep in the kind of little three-cornered room that was made in the hollow of the great walls where they were pierced by the slit windows. You could even curtain one or two of them off from the main room, and there was space enough for a light bed-frame with pillows like the one where Su was lying. Someone had tied a rush charm on to the head of it, an unending twist. It was queer how still and on there would be wee small tufts of swansdown floating around Su, floating and soft in the shadow, swirling suddenly in the draughts from the glassless windows, or shining momently in a sunbeam. But the feather dress that had been upon her, and that had fallen from her when she had stopped being a swan, that had been taken by the priest, tied safely with cords sealed with a cross marked seal, and laid in the bottom of the small chest behind the altar in the chapel where also were the holy vessels of beaten silver and gold, and the vestments for Easter and Christmas and the Days of the great saints. Su did not know of this, but Winkie knew.

He said to the priest, "In four days now yon green-mantled woman will keep her word and will be back. She is no friend to me or mine, and you will need to put me under a strong protection against her."

The priest said, "It could be better, son, if you left her to myself to deal with. If it is true that she is of evil and the swan-maid of good."

"That is of a high truth, Father," said Winkie very earnestly.

For a time the priest said nothing. At last he said, "Son, how do you know this? Have you seen the swan-maid in your life before?"

It seemed to Winkie very necessary that he should speak truth, since without truth he would not get protection. And yet it was the hardest kind of truth for another to believe, and the priest with his own kind of truth into which all others must be fitted. At last Winkie said, "I have seen her before in the time when she was not a swan, and she has a quest, and this quest is one which I must share."

"What is the quest of the swan-maid?" asked the priest.

"To find a young child that has been stolen by the kin of the green-mantled woman, and bring him back to gentle fostering."

"That could be a maiden's quest," said the priest thoughtfully, "but was it Themselves that turned her into a swan?"

"It could have been," said Winkie, and then wondered if this was right, for after all it must have been the Brounie. Away back in the time when Su was up at the Big House, and himself down in the village, and with the feeling always of half fright and half just not knowing which way the cat would jump—but the Brounie had come to him, too—ach, it was too difficult altogether to explain, yon!

Then a young man came in. He was not one of those that had been about in the castle, yet Winkie felt he knew him very well, and the name came to his lips. "Conn!" he said, and the young man nodded in a sidelong way, and made a kind of salute with his spear. And then it was to Winkie as though things were rushing back into his mind as a suddenly remembered dream does, from the days before he had taken the oath on the book with the mark on its cover. "Conn," he cried, "did you find them?" For he knew that Conn MacVurich, his foster brother, had been on a certain hunt, and three with him of the best of the young men, and the quarry—oh, oh, what Conn had hunted had been the murderers, the ones with whom he had the blood feud! And now he was trembling, horridly, and he minded on the look of his father's speared body, the torn and bruised flesh, and the blood spilled and no way at all to put it back.

Conn said, "We have found—something."

"Which?" said Winkie, and the knowledge on him that what had happened before was that there had been a raid, part of the other clan coming creeping up on a hunting party where his father might be separated from the rest of the men. And they had swooped and struck and ridden off, laughing, and it was only after Conn and his friends would have done a like thing that it could be undone. No, not that even, but revenged, made equal.

Conn said "Look!" And Winkie looked to the door of his castle, and there were two of his men dragging between them another, whose hands were tied behind him, and face spattered with blood and earth, the tartan draggled after him. They pulled him along, catching his feet in the rushes, and threw him down in front of Winkie who, knowing he was an enemy, breathed deep and laid his hand on the hilt of his own sword.

"It is a brother," said Conn. "We got him alone and brought him back for yourself to deal with. It will be better so."

"Aye," said Winkie, "it will be better." And he took a step forward, and the man huddled at his feet gave a queer little moan, and his arms jerked and twitched. But Winkie was thinking where to strike with the sword. He drew it, and tried its edge with his thumb, but it was scarcely sharp enough to cut the man's head even half off.

Words went through his mind about a sacrifice, a blood sacrifice. And the heaviness of the blood feud off himself. He began to walk round and round the man, dancing a little and balancing the sword in his hand. And met Su—Su in her long white nightgown, with the white bandage on her arm, and her hair half loose from its plaits. "You can't, Winkie!" she said. "You can't kill him!"

"I can, so," said Winkie.

"Not—not really! Oh Winkie, you aren't going to?"

"I am," said Winkie. "It is my enemy, and I have found him." He went past her, his eyes on the man who was now as still as though he had been dead.

And he was going to do it. Perhaps it didn't count, she thought, being in the past. And not really Winkie, but the one whose shape Winkie was wearing. But it was Winkie inside. He would have done it, he would have remembered having done it, so it had just got to count. It didn't somehow seem to matter about those people he had killed in battle. She hadn't been there anyhow, but now she was here, and she was responsible. She just had to be. If only the Brounie was here, she whispered to herself with an awful ache in her mind.

The others were all staring at her. Not only Winkie, but the lad Conn, and his friends, and the priest. And Conn covered his eyes, and one or two of them fell on their faces on the floor, and Winkie took a step towards her, and the priest was saying something in Latin.

For the sky had darkened suddenly behind her, the bright sun shafting blotted out of the slit windows, and a pattern of brightness came between herself and them, a pattern as huge as the hall, of a cross in a square, and the lines within the cross, and then the joining together of the lines through curves and loops. But as the lines came into one continuing line, all fell together, condensed into a bright rain of swansdown that floated and dropped, floated and dropped, around the swan-maid. And then again the sun shafts were tilting into the half dusk of the hall.

The priest said urgently to the young Chief, "Listen to her, son, she has laid a thing on you not to do."

Winkie said, "The blood feud was laid on me before she spoke."

Su said, "But there is another law above that. There must be!"

"Yes," said the priest, and took a step over to her, and held up his hand, facing the others, "*Thou shalt not kill.* That is the law above the blood feud. I have said this many times, maiden, but there was none to listen to me. It has been said to them and to their fathers, and to their fathers' fathers for long enough back, but still over this thing they will follow no law but the law of the old days."

"And the High Chief, the Lord of the Isles, what does he say?" Su was thinking hard.

"It is not in his hands," said the priest.

"Then it ought to be," said Su, "and it shall be. Winkie, this is just stupid! If you go and kill this man, then the blood feud goes on, and someone is going to kill you. Oh, can't you see? Can't you keep him prisoner, and take him to the Lord of the Isles, and have a proper trial and everything?"

"He is mine!" said Winkie, and he looked just like a dog if you try to take his bone away.

The man on the floor had lifted his head a little. He had been sick into the rushes. Conn shook Winkie and said in a loud voice, "Give him to her!"

"No!" said Winkie, but his voice was shaking a little, as Su remembered it had once at school when he had a row with the headmaster. He had been partly right, too. But all the same he got the strap.

She didn't want that now, she didn't want to see him bullied into a thing. She said, "Oh Winkie, please!" And then she knelt down in the rushes in front of him. It seemed somehow to be the right thing to do.

And Winkie gulped and said, "You're spoiling everything!" And then, "Well, go on. I suppose you've got to have him, and me to keep the blood feud on me!" He seemed to be awfully upset.

The priest said quick, "The man is yours, maiden. To whom do you give him until judgment of the High Chief?"

"To you," she said just as quickly. She didn't want him, the horrible messy creature, and she supposed the priest would have a bit of sense. Anyway, he looked pleased now, but Winkie didn't. They took the prisoner off to some kind of cage they had, in the bottom of the wall, with bars across it. After a lot of arguing between the priest and the rest of the men, they gave him straw and cushions to lie on, and food and water. She thought he'd be all right, but it all took a long time. And her arm was hurting again!

Winkie wouldn't speak to her. It was as if she had taken something of his that he wanted awfully, and when she said that the others in the castle all seemed to think it right, the way it had turned out, he said that they had just been scared of yon fireworks, but he himself had known that they were nothing but a sham. And then he went sulking off with Conn to shoot something, and left her with the women and the priest to talk to.

The worst of it was everyone was kind of half scared, and apt to say yes to her about everything. And anyhow she didn't know what to talk to them about. They were always being very busy. It was only very small children who ever really played. The slave women worked all the time. You had to have someone at the quern grinding meal all morning to get enough for everyone. The older women in the long embroidered dresses, who seemed to be related one way or another to the Chief, were doing weaving and embroidery, but when it was too dark they sang and played the harp, mostly long poems about people she had never heard of, and it seemed very dull, rather like a serial story when you don't know the beginning. Nobody read any books, and nobody knew any-

thing about the rest of the world. They seemed to be
frightened of an awful lot of things, and they kept on trying to bring themselves luck, taking any amount of
trouble about it, and sometimes Su thought it would have
been easier, as well as more sensible, to work a bit harder,
and think a little more.

But it was no good her saying that. It didn't fit into
their minds. They put down anything odd she said, to her
being a swan-maid. And the same with the things she
couldn't do. For instance, the oldest of the women, who
seemed to be Winkie's father's sister, offered to let her
embroider with the gold and silver threads and the box of
bored seed pearls which were used for the very best
things. But it wasn't Su's line at all! So when they saw she
couldn't do it, they were all awfully sorry for her and
said, "She will have forgotten the bower crafts in the
time when she was a swan." And they fussed over her as
though it were something dreadful. Her arm was now
practically healed. It had skinned over and didn't hurt
unless she knocked it against something. But the priest
still put some lovely smelling stuff on to it and bandaged
it fresh every day.

He wasn't quite so difficult to talk to. At first he seemed
like the sort of grown-ups Su was used to in her own
times. He was really awfully kind, and he told her a lot
about flowers and plants and what one could do with
them, and he had lots of lovely adventure stories, mostly
about saints, but not soppy saints; in fact, you wouldn't
know they were saints at all, they were always fighting or
doing magic or making friends with animals. But then he
would suddenly say something so queer that she was
quite sure his mind was away different inside. That was
always rather frightening and reminded her of how far
away she really was.

He asked her a lot of questions about the time before

she was a swan, which she found quite easy to answer, because naturally he didn't ask her questions about railway trains and aeroplanes and Esse stoves, so she didn't have to bring them in. She explained that she lived in a big house with lots of rooms with fires and tables and cushions, yes, and rugs on the floor and pictures on the walls. There were small tapestries on the walls of the women's rooms, the bower they called it, and one in the big room behind the Chief's chair, where Winkie sat on red-leather cushions. It had the queerest-looking stags on it and as little like as could be to the great-great-grand-mothers in the heavy gold frames or the modern colour prints at home in the Big House. The priest asked her if she was a princess. She shook her head; but all the same she knew he had got that idea into his head because of all the rooms and fires and furnishings. She told him about the flowers in the garden, and he just loved that; he said it was like the gardens of paradise surely; but when he asked her how many cows there were and she answered three, he just smiled and looked at her as if she couldn't count. He asked her if she had been in church or chapel, and she said yes. Then he put her through a kind of scripture exam rather like school, only it was mostly New Testament, and they hadn't done that so much as Old Testament and psalms at the Port-na-Sgadan school. She could read out the Latin more or less from his book, but she couldn't translate it except a word here or there. Still he seemed awfully pleased and surprised that she could read, and even more determined that she was a princess. He didn't give her any arithmetic questions. Perhaps he didn't know much himself.

He did ask her about her quest. At first she didn't know what he meant; then she saw that Winkie must have told him about Donald. So she explained about her winning of Donald. It was comforting in a way that he believed everything she said, and yet in a way it was worrying, too. A proper grown-up wouldn't have believed it. Anyway, he said he'd do his best to help her.

Mostly they talked in the chapel. It was a wee small place, and dark, but Su liked it all the same. It smelt of incense instead of stale food and dogs and smoke. The services were in Latin, but there was no sermon. There were several things hung up on the walls, including a great huge sword with a nick on the blade; she never found out who that had belonged to.

It seemed to be nearly a week now since she had been in the castle. And still Winkie was away hunting. They were speaking of stags and wild boars and wolves. It must be good fun for him, she thought, being almost a grown-up, having this skill that must have been in the hands and body of the young Chief whom he had become, able to go off riding and hunting and rushing round whenever he wanted to, instead of still being at school. He wouldn't like going back. And when he did? Would he some way remember how to ride and shoot with a bow and swing a sword with both hands like he could now? And what would be the good of it in their real time even if he did remember? He'd never get the chance. This was the life for Winkie, all right! It would make Port-na-Sgadan school look pretty silly. And even the fishing. Suppose he didn't want to go back?

The priest kept going up to the very top of the castle, where the spiral stair in the corner of the great wall opened on to a roof of heavy stone slates pegged on to the sarking across the roof-beams. There was plenty of room to walk round on the tops of the outer walls. It must have been an awful job to build, she thought, dragging these great stones up with no proper machinery, cranes and chains and things, not even saws for the beams, but only axes! She asked the priest how long it had been built, but all he said was that it had been there first long, long ago, in the time of the saints. But nobody seemed to bother whether things that were over had happened a few years ago or hundreds. They aren't so fussy about time as we are, thought Su, and maybe it's better that way.

She had asked the priest if she could come up with him. He didn't say yes at once. But at last he did. She went over to the parapet and looked down. She thought the river had some different bends in it, but the shape of the coast was about the same. It made her feel home-sick and a bit dizzy. She stepped back from the parapet and put her hands over her eyes. Suddenly she felt the priest's hands on her shoulders. He said, "Is there fear on you?"

"It's just the way I feel giddy. It's so high up," she said, and gulped.

He said low in her ear, "But you could fly. Fly, now!"

She shook her head, "No! No, I can't! No!" She was suddenly frightfully scared in case he'd try to throw her off the roof and she wriggled round and held on to him tight.

He was quite gentle, though. He stroked her forehead and said, "You are no swan, then, but all maiden now?"

She said, "Yes! Yes, of course," and he nodded.

He kept on looking north towards the thick forest, and then in a little he pointed, and said, "See, they are coming!" She looked, and there, still a long way off on the forest path she could see several people riding, and one of them must be Winkie. There was a little bright glitter from spear-points or the jingly bits on the horses' harness. Then they were into the shadow of the forest again. The priest said, "This is the seventh day since the green-mantled woman appeared to us first." Then he looked at Su.

She said, "Do you think—do you think truly she will come again?"

"Yes," said the priest, "and I must be there with the young Chief. Will you come with me, maiden, and maybe we will get word of your own quest?"

"Oh please!" she said anxiously, and suddenly afraid that Winkie mightn't be able to manage by himself. She did wish she knew if the Brounie was anywhere about.

She went with the priest into the chapel and saw him take a cross off the altar and hang it round his own neck. He put another on to hers; it was made of gold with a pattern all over it, a little like the pattern the Brounie had made. Then he filled a covered silver cup with water out of the great cup at the door. He was talking to himself in Latin all the time, and she didn't like to ask questions.

Then he called one of the women to bring her shoes and a mantle. She had mostly gone barefoot in the castle. They fetched a pair of soft deerskin brogues and a long white woollen mantle with fur trimmings and a clasp of heavy silver and enamel. Like everything else she had been given to wear, it was much longer than she liked; you couldn't run in those sort of clothes, not unless you kilted them up to the knee like Fair Janet in the ballad. It was funny thinking of Fair Janet again just then. But she got Tam Lin back from the Fairy Queen.

> *Then out and spoke the Fairy Queen*
> *Out of a bush of broom,*
> *She that has gotten young Tam Lin*
> *Has gotten a stately groom.*
>
> *And out and spoke the Fairy Queen*
> *And an angry woman was she——*

But was the green-mantled woman the same as the Fairy Queen? Could she be? Was she really going to appear? Su stood at the door of the castle and got hold of the mantle and robe in both hands so that she wouldn't trip over them. The mantle had no pockets, of course. That was just one of the annoying things, not having pockets for anything. But then nobody had any hankies either, and no money, nor pencils, nor toffees, nor bits of string, nor any of the kind of things one does have in one's pockets. It would be miserable in winter if everyone caught colds, and they were sure to with all the draughts!

She and the priest went down the steps of the castle together. It was a lovely day, the kind of summer day when nothing nasty ought to happen. There were some small rough cattle about, rather like Highlanders but not quite so much so. There were some goats and a few sheep and little brown hens. Everything smelt lovely. They went on down the path that led into the forest. And at last they heard the voices of the riders a bit ahead of them.

Chapter XII

THE GREEN-MANTLED WOMAN

———————————

Winkie had killed a wolf, a killer of men and of
beasts. He had speared it through the throat,
a clean cast. It had been a wonderful proud,
happy thing. Conn had made a song about it, and they
sang it round the fire that evening, praising their young
Chief. That had put out the sore thought of what Su had
done on him; he was not minding on Su. He went over
in his head the first sight of the wolf, uneasy and angry
and snarling enmity, and it coming nearer, nearer, and
the spear lifted, the moment of uncertainty and the great
moment of certainty. That kept on repeating beautifully
like the great music, the *Ceol Mór*.

He was still turning it over and over in his mind as they
rode through the forest. The led horses were dragging a
kind of sled with the bodies of two deer and a small wild
pig, and the skin of his own wolf. The dogs kept on sniffing at it whenever they stopped. Wherever the trees
thinned out there would be young birch and flowers and
broom bushes and small birds flitting about. Out of a
broom bush the green-mantled woman rose in front of
him and his horse stopped with its four feet planted and
ears pricked forward. Conn made a peculiar noise out of
the back of his throat, and said, "It is the seventh day!"

Yon first time he had seen her Winkie had thought her

terrible bonny, more than the bonniest lassie on the cover of any book down at the wee paper shop, or in any picture at the picture-house even. She was like the lassie who had been his partner for the reel down under in the hill yon time. But this one was not young. If he could have reached her, have taken her hand, she could have told him—have told him—everything. And she was here again. And yet his enemy. He could not hold that steady in his mind because of yon great beauty coming at him like the hot golden smell off the broom bush.

She said, in a voice that was quite soft, yet clear, like a blackbird's singing, "Oh welcome to the wolf-killer, welcome to the Chief! Great spear casts and bow-shots to you always!" But he had missed with his bow-shot aiming at the swan's breast, eye glance along the straight arrow. If he had shot the swan all would have been well, the blood feud off him now. Nothing to make him think he was, maybe, not the Chief in truth, but only wee Winkie from the village school. That was a dream. That was a dream. His horse was moving slowly towards the broom bush, and the woman with the honey voice. And suddenly he knew the bewitched treason in his thought—how he was wanting Su not to be there, Su to be killed, Su not ever to come back on him! He lifted his right hand with the boar spear, and cast fiercely at the broom bush.

But the green-mantled woman put up her hand and caught the spear as though it had been a light flower. "I thank you for the love gift, wolf killer!" she said, "And you will see me yet again." At that there came a horror on them all. For she was armed, and maybe she would turn it against them. She need not touch the cold iron of the blade, only the ashwood shaft. But she turned and stepped away from them with a laughing look, half over one shoulder.

The Green-Mantled Woman

The horses were snorting and refusing in a lather with fear. They would not move until the green mantle was almost out of sight at the bend in the path ahead. Winkie steadied his horse with hands and knees, then reached across to loose his sword in the scabbard. He knew his men were behind him, ready to back him: brave, armed, his friends. The horses were trotting now with a cheery jingle and clatter. There ahead was the green mantle flickering between the green, flower-speckled forest banks.

The small horses trotted harder. Round the corner. And there was the green-mantled woman standing against an oak tree, the boar spear dropped at her feet, her white hands covering her face, and at one side of her the priest and at the other side Su, each holding up a cross against her.

Winkie jumped clear of the horse and had his sword half drawn, when the priest cried out, "I have her ringed with the holy water, do not you break the ring, son!" Su looked round at Winkie. He nodded at her. But he seemed to be looking far off, still; she didn't like to say anything. The priest spoke again. "She is in your power now, son, if there is anything you would ask of her." When Winkie still said nothing, but looked queerly at the woman, he went on, "It could be that if I were to give her a slashing with the holy water she would vanish in smoke."

Su said suddenly, imploringly, "Ask her about Donald, Winkie! Oh please!"

Winkie jumped a little, as though her voice had woke him up somehow, and he shoved back his sword into the scabbard with a hard rattle. He said loudly to the woman, "Where is Donald Ferguson?"

The woman said nothing, but slowly dropped her hands from her face and smiled and shook her head. "Go on, Winkie!" said Su.

"Tell me", said Winkie, "or else——" He signed to the priest, who lifted the silver cup and threw a few drops of water on his finger-tips towards the woman, who suddenly gave a most horrid scream, as though it had really burnt her.

Su ducked and screwed up her eyes, and her hands went up to her ears. But Winkie sat forward on his horse and stared. The priest was speaking in Latin. Conn and the other men were kneeling with the horses' bridles caught in their clasped hands. The woman held out her white arms towards Winkie. "What do you want of me, wolf-killer? Power, knowledge of the stars, the speech of birds? Only keep your servant from me!"

The priest looked at Winkie, who shook his head. "You know I am not taking your gifts," he said to the woman. "I want the one thing. You had best tell quick."

"You do not want me for your enemy," said the woman.

"I am not taking you for my enemy," said Winkie.

"We only want to know about Donald," said Su suddenly. "Oh please, we aren't your enemies really."

But the priest was between them, speaking in Latin, and that seemed to be doing something to the woman. It was as though the colour in her face and the colour in her mantle had both faded a little. All at once she spoke. "The body of Donald Ferguson is asleep in the Big House in time to come. But the soul of Donald Ferguson is in this time under the stone of the Boar, and it is shaped like a golden hazel nut."

"What is that stone?" said Winkie.

"You will be going to the place of it," she said. "It is by that you will know I speak truth." And her voice had gone higher and some way far off. "Let me go now."

The priest said, "She is of evil. She should be destroyed."

Winkie didn't answer him. He said to Su, "She has

144

spoken, and this is what you are after, but all the same she tried to make me kill you."

"Oh, it doesn't matter!" said Su, jumping from one foot to the other. "Don't let's do anything more! Oh Winkie, let's go and look for this stone at once and then go home."

"I have it half in my mind that I know what yon stone is, that I have touched yon stone," said Winkie, and frowned.

Then from behind Conn said, "It is the stone of Dun Add surely, the old ancient stone, and in truth you have touched it and your fathers before you."

"The stone of Dun Add," said Winkie. "But I am not wanting to go to Dun Add."

"It is there you will be going for all that," said the woman in her shrunken voice. "Let me go now."

"Yes," said Winkie.

"No!" said the priest, and put his hand to the silver cup. But Winkie took him by the arm.

"It is best to keep faith, even with the other world," he said. "Go in peace now." He walked his horse across the ring of holy water, and as he did it the woman gave a cry and lifted her hands above her head like a diver, and seemed to dive straight upwards into the branches of the oak. As she went through the leaves there was a great, sudden sound of singing and the baying of hounds, and then silence, like a slammed door.

"It is my hope that you have not done ill, my son," said the priest.

"There was nothing else it was right for me to do," said Winkie, and then, "Su, look at my wolf! I speared him myself. He was coming at me."

"Oh Winkie!" said Su, and he was well pleased with the feel of her voice, and she stared at the wolf-skin, and then back at him, the way he wanted.

"Come on up behind me," he said. "Is your arm better? That's grand now."

She tried to pull herself up on to the horse, but her silly clothes got in the way. Then one of the men gave her a hoist, and she was up, feeling rather wobbly and holding on to Winkie. It came to her mind now how thin he had been yon other time outside the Big House, but now he seemed terrible strong and solid, the sort of person who might easily kill a wolf. And he wasn't cross with her any longer. "Are there many wolves?" she asked.

"Aye, a fair few," said Winkie, "but there is one less now." He told her again as they rode through the green summer forest just how it had been, and she listened the way he wanted her to listen. Across the glen they heard the sound of tinkling and saw two men carrying a bar of metal on a kind of wooden stretcher. "The tinklers at their work," said Winkie, "but it is best not to be asking overmuch."

"Are they making things?" asked Su.

"Aye," said Winkie. "All of our swords and spearheads and everything that is in it for a fighter, and cooking pots and pans forby that."

"Don't you make any yourselves?"

"Ach no, it is always them, and it was so always. They are different from ourselves. They know all the red earths and how to work with them, and they are hither and thon, not settled in houses nor under any chief except, maybe, for a short protection. When we have bought from these ones, they will be gone."

He was speaking to her over his shoulder, and while he spoke Su got a quick sight between birch trees of some girls breaking sticks. One of them looked up, and she was sure enough 'Dina, and she nodded quickly with a small flash of a smile just the same way 'Dina might have been if she had seen Su not alone but with someone else from Port-na-Sgadan that she couldna be too sure of.

When they were near the house one of the men came running out to tell Winkie that there was a letter. He seemed put about over it, and Su began teasing him about the post being late, and then shut up because it looked as if that would make him cross again. She slipped off at the door, feeling rather stiff, and followed him in.

Winkie knew the letter was from the High Chief, the Lord of the Isles. He did not want the letter. He did not want to be bothered to bits or have to make up his mind. It had been kind of nice in the wood with Su, and the great thought of his wolf at the back of his mind. And the thought that he had gone the right way about with yon fairy woman, and had neither made her a friend nor yet an enemy. He had shown himself to be truly the Chief. And Su wasna doubting him. But this letter would be from the one who was over him, and it would mean he would have one thing or another laid on him to do, and that not of his own choosing. Yet it had got to be done, just the same way his own folk needed to do what he himself said.

The High Chief's messenger was standing in the hall, the jar of wine waiting to be poured. Winkie drank from the flat quaich of polished maple wood bound with clear gold and gave the cup to the messenger, who drank too in the name of his Chief. They spoke gravely of this and that, and Winkie would suddenly mind on something from further back in this life, jumping up through his thought like a trout out of dark water, and once it had become plain he could go on to speak of it. At last they spoke of the letter, and the messenger took it out from the breast of the plaid. It was rolled and tied, with a grand noble seal to it with the mark on it of the High Chief's ring. Before all his men Winkie broke the seal and unrolled the letter. It was written with fine curly words of Latin, the speech of those that do not think common thoughts, nor in common words. Winkie frowned over it, and Su came to look over his shoulder. They made out a word or two between them. It was queer, Su thought, how Winkie now knew Latin the way he had never known it before. She had been a bit swanky to him in her letter from the English school about learning Latin. Now he knew more than she did. It was like the riding and shooting and all. She didn't quite like him being better than herself at a thing like Latin. But most of this was beating him anyway!

Then the priest came back. He read through the letter in Latin, aloud, and Winkie understood. It was bidding him to come to a gathering of the Council at the old gathering place at Dun Add. "It was truth then the green woman spoke," said Winkie.

"And then we'll get Donald's soul and be able to go back!" said Su.

But Winkie didn't answer. He was thinking of something else. He said to the priest, "We will take the prisoner, and the High Chief will make a judgment." Then he gave orders that all was to be made ready for a start the next day.

They began the journey in the morning, with a lot of fuss and shouting and people rushing about. They were all riding on the little horses, but Su had a carved wooden saddle like a small chair. It wasn't exactly comfortable, but it was easier than sitting behind someone and holding on all the time. The prisoner was having to ride a led horse, with his hands tied behind him. He looked to be in a terrible mess and fright still, and whenever they could the men would hit him or jerk his tied arms. Su tried to speak to him sometimes, but he only answered in a whisper and she didn't quite know what to say. Winkie didn't

even look at him. There were a couple of pack-horses
with food and a cooking pot and warm furs to lie on at
night, for it took them two days. The way they went was
not at all the road that the buses were to go on later. Their
road went along by the coast almost all the time, and it
was hardly a road, more the kind of path sheep make.
The horses were strung out all along it.

They camped in the evening and made a fire. Su
wanted to talk to Winkie, but it was difficult with the
men all round him. At last one of them unwrapped a small
kind of harp that he had been carrying on his back and
began to play, and while the music went on Su got
edging closer to Winkie. She said, "What will we do
when we get to Dun Add, Winkie?"

'We will need to see what the High Chief wants of us,"
said Winkie.

"But we will look for the stone of the Boar, won't we?"

"I have it in my mind where the stone is," Winkie
answered.

"Have you been there?"

"Aye, in this life."

"But will we find it at once? To-morrow, Winkie?"

"Well, we will see what the High Chief says."

"But I am so afraid all this is taking up real time. It
feels like it."

"It *is* real!" said Winkie suddenly and fiercely, almost
as if he was hitting her. The men were singing a song now,
the song about the young Chief who had killed the wolf.
She didn't say any more until it was finished, but she was
feeling rather frightened.

At last she said, "Winkie, are you feeling cross at me
still about the prisoner?" He didn't answer. She went on,
"I'm just sure you would have felt bad afterwards if you
had killed him."

"I would not," said Winkie.

She floundered on, the fear growing in her. "Winkie, you are coming back with me, aren't you?"

"Ach," said Winkie, "I canna tell you that, Su, and you had best not be asking me," and he called to the harper for another tune.

Su didn't get to sleep for a long time that night. She was hashing and fashing in her mind over Winkie and him liking it so well here that he wanted to stay, and she could see just the very way it must be and how could she blame him. But to leave her! How could he be wanting to leave her? And it might be for ever. As if he was dead. And what would his father and mother say, and what could she say herself? Oh dear, oh dear. She only wanted to be back. She was aching quite a lot, partly from sitting in the wooden saddle, and partly in her arm. The scar was still very red and tickly. She cried and cried, taking care that the men didn't hear, and wasn't at all comforted, even when she noticed that the stars were the same as in her own time. That just seemed silly.

Chapter XIII

THE STONES OF DUN ADD

n the morning she felt better. The Brounie would see
them past, surely! Everyone was cheery enough, except the prisoner. He still half thought he was going
to be killed. Su began to think they were all being so horrible to him just to stop themselves being nice by accident.
She fed him with porridge at breakfast, and they pretended not to see. Then they rode on. She could tell more
or less where they were by the shape of the coast. They
had got back to where the road used to be—no, was
going to be. And sometimes there would be a few huts at
the foot of the burns where there was good grass and
shelter, in the very same places the houses were when
you passed on the bus. She used to think the buses were
awfully jolty, but this saddle was away worse. Yet it
almost made her cry again thinking of the buses, and the
road, and coming home from school, and how far off it
all seemed now.

They saw plenty of deer, big red ones mostly, and
hares and foxes and badgers, otters at work by the stream,
and small furry bright-eyed creatures in the trees that
were like what Su had read about in books about Canada.
The only thing she didn't see were rabbits. The animals

were all going about their business, and she got the feeling that the people were only visitors, or rather as if they were all part of the same animals' world. Once they saw some footmarks in a boggy patch, and the men were excited and said it was a bear, and twice they heard a great squeaking and grunting, and eight or ten baby pigs came rustling through the ferns and hazels, with a big bristly mother pig looking after them. Summer was baby time for all the wild ones. There were fawns running with the deer, and fox cubs and fluffy broods of wild duck, and grouse and partridges. The men were friendly with them, would race to catch a wild baby, and then let it go. All day there was hot sun, and the smell of honeysuckle in the woods, or heather in the open.

Once, near a clearing, and a circle of houses, they heard a tinkling and smelt fire. And there were the leather-aproned folk working their bronze and iron. They had stopped a while there, for men and horses to drink, for girths to be loosed, and a piece to be cut off the barley loaf with the dirk. Su was wanting to pick flowers in the edge of the wood, and she was at it when a lassie came stepping down from the far side of the burn with a wooden coggie to fill. Su stared at her, "'Dina!" she said, "what at all are you doing here?"

The lassie gave a wee smile, the same kind of one-sided way that 'Dina had, and said, "So it's yourself, and indeed you are far enough from your own place."

"I know," said Su sadly.

The lassie was kneeling at the far side, her hair just touching the water. She spoke softly across the water, "Dinna greet now. You are on your way surely."

"Aye," said Su, snivelling a bit. "How do you know?"

"*She* tellt me," said the 'Dina lassie kneeling back on her heels, and taking out from the neck of her dress the very same fairy flower.

The Stones of Dun Add

Something puzzled Su. How could it be the same one she had seen two days before when they themselves had been riding hard to get here? "'Dina, is it you here, the same as I saw when I was a swan? And the same as I saw in the wood with Winkie, too?"

"Ach, well," said the lassie, standing up with the full coggie dripping. "You shouldna be asking such questions, for they are terrible ill to answer." She went away to the wood at the far side towards the tapping and clinking of anvils. Su felt a bittie cheered up over this, and she wanted to tell Winkie. But he was not wanting to be with her much. He wanted to be with the young men. They rode on along the coast. Su thought by the look of it they must be at the foot of Loch Fyne. Yes, it must be Ardrishaig: but no lock gates and no harbour with fishing boats. Only a small stone and timber castle, and some houses, and sheep and cattle, herded by half-bare children. Winkie and his gang seemed to know everyone here, and it was the same tartan on them all, and after a lot of talk they all rode on together. She could hear the new ones asking about the swan-maid and pointing at her, but nobody spoke to her. She wondered if they were frightened of her. It was a lonely kind of feeling.

In the evening the sun was going down behind high hills, but they themselves had come out into flat country with patches of bog and a river running through it. Here, there were more people all riding to and fro, and the bright tartans against the slowly darkening green.

They came to a small steep hill with a rocky peak beside a loop of the broad river. People were beginning to light fires and camp all round it. Winkie reined in his horse and spoke to Conn. And Su, as usual, was left wondering what it was all about. At last Winkie came to her and said, "This is Dun Add."

"Oh," said Su, "and the stone? Is it here, Winkie?"

"Aye," he said, and then, "Do you want to look for it, Su? I will if you want, but——"

"We could see if it's there still, couldn't we?" she said. "Then I'd know!"

"Ach, Su," said Winkie, "I wish—well, I suppose it has just got to be this way, but if only it hadn't to be!" He seemed terrible put about, but Su didn't notice much. She was so pleased to be off the horse and on her feet again.

"Come on, Winkie," she said, and tugged at his hand.

They began to climb the hill. There were men in chain-mail shirts, with plaids over them, and great spears and swords and shields of iron with spikes and queer beasts painted and gilt. They seemed to know Winkie, and passed him on, and they stared at Su, who felt a good bit affronted and wishing it was all over. It was late on, too, and once in a while she couldn't keep from yawning. It must be almost night, but there was a moon in it, and here and there the bright moving glare of a torch.

They went up stone steps and through a long narrow stone entrance, a scary kind of place. Now they seemed to be in a sort of fort with wooden houses and stables and shelters. "Do you know it, Winkie?" whispered Su.

And he answered, "Aye, I kind of half know it with the inside of me."

Still they went up, passing a great door of iron-studded oak, which clanged behind them. Here they were taken by one of the guards into a wooden hall, high beamed, with woven hangings, and in the middle a great flaming fire that threw them into a warm dazzle. Out of the dark a man with a gold-coloured beard and hair, and gold on his head and arms, came over to them and Winkie knelt on one knee and held the hilt of his sword for the man to touch. Su didn't know what she was supposed to do, but thought it couldn't do any harm to make a proper dancing class curtsey. The man put his arms round Winkie's shoulders and took him off to the table where there was lots to eat, and golden cups to drink from.

After a while two women came and took Su by the hands and brought her over to the other end of the table where the women were, all with grand embroidered over-dresses above fine white shirts, and all with linen head-dresses, starched or ironed into wings or trailing behind them. They gave Su lots to eat, especially a kind of squashy cake made with honey and cream, and then one of them undid her plaits and began to comb her hair very gently with an ivory comb. She was getting awfully sleepy, and still Winkie was talking to the High Chief.

At last he came over. He was as pleased as a peacock. "Su," he said, "my Chief will take the prisoner himself, and he will clear the whole thing and take the blood feud off me. Ach, Su, the light I feel to have that promised!"

"He isn't going to kill the man, is he?" said Su anxiously. The whole thing had been such a muddle, and she didn't like the man, but all the same she had got it fixed in her mind that he wasn't to be killed.

"No, no, not at all!" said Winkie. "But there will be a judgment from the judgment seat, and a thing will be laid on my enemies instead of the life, and the thing which was laid on me will be taken off. And after that we will not be enemies. It is a terrible thing, Su, to have the blood crying on one."

"And what about the stone?" she said. "Did you ask him?"

"Aye, aye, we spoke of yourself and your quest, but better we should wait till morning, because the stone of the Boar is the old stone of crowning, and there could be spirits there that would not maybe like to be woken at night."

"I did hope we could go back to-night," she said.

The Stones of Dun Add

"Well, it will be away better by daylight, Su—and I swear on the iron I will take you to it, Su!" he added suddenly and surprisingly.

"Of course you will," she said. "What is the matter anyway, Winkie?"

"Ach, nothing," he said, and he gave her a small shove and went back to his own end of the table. The nice women who had been combing Su's hair took her along to a room at the back of the hall, where there were feather beds as soft as clouds. There was hardly time to begin worrying about Winkie before she was fast asleep.

Winkie woke her out of deep dreams. "Come now," he said urgently, "before everyone is about."

She rubbed her eyes and shook herself. In a few minutes they were out of the hall on the short trodden turf between the walls of the inner fort. The ground rose so that they could see above the stone and turf dykes to where the river Add went wandering west to the sea, and the blue islands. It was high tide now, and there were boats tied up to a jetty. One of them had two small brown sheep in it, tied to the thwarts. When one of the sheep lifted its head and bleated they heard it very plainly in the stillness. They came to the two stones, first the stone of the footmark. "It was here", said Winkie, "that the High King stood to take the oath to the people in the days of the Kingdom of Dalriada."

Su began to say something, and then she saw the second stone, the stone of the Boar, with the Boar's outline carved on it. If she stared at it any longer, she knew she was going to get awfully frightened. There was nothing for it but to go ahead. She dropped on her knees beside the stone, and began to dig with her fingers. "Do you really want to, Su?" said Winkie suddenly.

"Of course I do," she said, and he handed her his dirk. She stuck it in hard, and the point grated on something.

She cut through the turf, and there was a box and the lid was carved with knotted lines like the inside part of the pattern the Brounie had drawn. She lifted the lid, and within was the golden hazel nut.

"Well," she said, "so that's all right." She shut the lid down. And then, "We can go back any time."

Winkie looked at her. "Yes," he said, "we could."

She sat back on her heels, holding on to the box. Somehow, she had never thought it would be so easy. She had been half sure there would be a catch somewhere. But, as she looked at Winkie, she began to know there was a catch after all. But not the kind of catch she had thought of. Something different and much harder to deal with. "Winkie," she said, "don't you want to go back?"

"I am not going back," he said very quietly. Somehow she knew he meant it, and that was that. And this wasn't like the fairy hill, where they both awfully much wanted to stay and yet knew they had got to go. This was a whole lot realler. It was as real as—now. And Winkie was never going back to Port-na-Sgadan school, and the tuppenny comics and the fizzy lemonade and going to the fishing when he was big, and getting like all the rest of them. She would go back and time would go on again. Her time, without Winkie.

"I suppose I have got to go by myself, then," she said slowly, and looked up at him and the folds of the plaid dropping from the silver brooch, and his hand on the hilt of his great sword. He said nothing. She went on talking to herself, to tell herself it was all right. "I came here on my wings," she said, "my swan wings. I suppose I will have to get back the same way. Winkie, oh Winkie, what happened to my feathers?"

Winkie looked down at her, and then suddenly he was kneeling on the turf beside her. "Su," he said, "Ach, my soul, your swan feathers were given to the priest, and he, thinking to keep you here as a mortal maid, he burned them. He meant to do right by you, Su, surely, but—but——"

"Oh, then I'll never get home!" said Su, and she threw herself down on the turf and sobbed and howled and almost burst with misery and anger. At last she began to stop. Winkie was trying to talk to her. He looked awfully worried. He said, "Even if you can't go back, I will see you are all right, Su, I swear to you—on my sword—oh Su, I will do anything at all! Look, I will marry you as soon as you say."

Su stopped crying suddenly. "I don't want to marry you, Winkie," she said. "I want to go home, and I'm jolly well going to go home some way or another, and none of this is real!"

"It is real to me," said Winkie.

"Well, I don't care what you say, it isn't! And you let your priest do that on me."

"I would have stopped him if I had known in time," said Winkie gravely, "even if it had cost me my soul or him his life."

"I think", said Su, and her voice was very trembly, "that the very best thing would be if the Brounie was to come." She looked down at the box. "That's the middle part of the inside of his pattern," she said, and she began to run her fingers along it.

The Brounie was standing between the stone of the Boar and the stone of the footmark. "Well," he said, "it's a sair fankle ye're in, the two of ye. And I am no' just sure o' the way out."

"Oh," said Su, "I am so glad you've come at last!" And she sniffed. "I want to go home."

"You canna gang the same gait you went," said the Brounie, "and that means that you canna gang your lane."

"But Winkie isn't coming," said Su.

"Then," said the Brounie, "here you maun stay, the

two of ye, for there's nothing I can do, nothing ava, and I had best be away afore folks are wakening."

"Oh no," said Su, "you can't leave us! I must go home, I must, I must, and I've got Donald's soul and everything, and oh it isn't fair!"

She was shivering and jumping now with rage and fear, and an awful kind of upside-down feeling. She turned on Winkie. "You promised I'd be all right, you promised on your sword, and now look at you!"

Then Winkie went very white, and he said, "No one shall say I am an oath-breaker. I will go back with you if that is the only way."

For a minute they stared at one another, and then Su began to cry again. "I didn't mean to hurt you, Winkie," she said. She was half doubled up as if she had a pain, with her left hand holding to the box and the right to Winkie's dirk.

"Nor I you," he said very gently. And then, to the Brounie, in a kind of awful despair, "Can I no' keep anything?"

"There is not one single thing you can keep, *a laoch*; you will gang bare as a bond slave for your lassie's sake. But this I can tell you: gif you are wanting them later and yourself a man grown, a' will be yours again."

Winkie looked hard at the Brounie, and the Brounie nodded. And then, from white, Winkie began to go red. He started to speak, and then stopped. At last he said: "Are you saying that truly? Will I have sword and bow, will I have the horses and the wine cups?"

"Aye, or as good."

"Will I have the Gaelic on my tongue and the songs made over me?"

"Fine you will hae that, my mannie."

"Will I have the leadership of men, and the friendship of the one that is my Chief?"

"A' that will be your's, gif you are wanting it truly. But it is on yourself to keep the living wish safe in your breast," said the Brounie gravely. The hill seemed terribly quiet round them, quiet and waiting on the Stone of the Boar.

"I wish," said Winkie, "I wish——"

"Dinna wish the noo," said the Brounie, "for it's ower late, but put you your hand by your lassie's hand, and both on the wee box, and tak tent o' yourselves and it. And when you are near to the Big House what is sleeping within will awaken and syne you will let it flee back into the breast of the wee fellow, and a' that's ill shall be well."

"Now?" said Winkie shakenly.

"Aye, now, and you sae fu' o' courage and vir!"

Winkie blinked, and suddenly put both hands hard down on to the box over Su's left hand, holding so tight that Su cried out. But her cry was lost in darkness and buffeting of great wings and gripping of great hands, and aye and on the sound of water falling. And Winkie held tight to the box and to Su's hand, but once Su struck out with her right hand and the dirk in it, and there came a kind of eldritch cry and a thing letting go, and then the darkness steadied into moon and stars, and the two looking at one another and the wee box between them.

Chapter XIV

TIMES WITHIN TIMES

"Are you all right, Winkie?" Su whispered.

"I'm fine," he said, "but where in all the world are we, Su?"

She looked round. Then she stood up, and suddenly noticed she was back in her blue pyjamas. She could see over to the river, shining in the moon. "I think," she said, "oh Winkie, I think we're still there."

Winkie didn't speak for a moment. He was feeling about himself, and Su could see that he was in an old jersey and shorts. "I should have a flash on me", he said, "if we are back in our own time. Aye, there it's." He flicked at it with his thumb, and gave it a shake to settle the battery. It clicked on, shining on Su, on grass, on stones, on one stone with lines on it, the fierce narrow head of a boar. "Aye," he said, "this is where we are. *The River Add is the biggest river in Argyll.* There was a thing they learnt us for the Qualifying. But God alone knows just *where* it is!"

"It was two-days' ride," said Su, "and—and I'm in my pyjamas! And I had an awfully nice white mantle with fur——"

"If you are minding on your braws," said Winkie, "it was fine gold I had on me. And my sword. Ach, Su, Su, I canna hardly bear to think on it."

"Winkie dear," said Su, "oh look, I've still got your dirk!" She held it out in her right hand. He seized on it.

"Ach, Su, aren't you the clever one! Aye, it's mine's." He ran his finger along the blade, and suddenly drew it back. "Gosh, Su, what at all were you doing with it? Yon's blood." He shone the torch on it. "It's no', it's green it is. But it's awful like blood. Could it be—could it be Themselves bleeding green, Su?"

"I don't know," she said, shivering and backing away from it. "I did stick it into something, and the box is safe——"

Winkie was thinking hard. "We turned into the tail of the day about where Ardrishaig would be, and we rode maybe an hour. That would have been north-west. We will need to go south-east, Su, if we're to get back to our own place. Isn't it devilish altogether the way the moon is putting the stars out? I could make a course on them, but I dinna ken what time of night it is, nor where the moon will be." He looked out. "Can you mind, Su, where it is yon river comes out? Is it Lochgilphead or Crinan? Look now, would yon be the canal? If it is, we could make our way to it, and maybe get a lift on a coal boat."

"But we've got back into our own time and it's going on, I know it is, I can feel it! And we wouldn't get home till day, and I'm in my pyjamas!"

"Ach, dinna be daft," he said impatiently, but Su had gone to the other side, and was looking down.

"Oh," she said, "there's a cock crowing. Oh, I do hope that doesn't mean it's morning!"

Winkie came and stood by her and listened, "Aye, there he goes! And the meaning is there's a farm, and maybe a farm road. Ach, come on, Su." He pulled her after him, and they went stumbling down the hill. At last they seemed to be on some kind of track. He shone the flash on it, and all of a sudden the farm buildings were black in front of them. Now the road was hard and knobbly on their bare feet. They went on along it, not saying a word. Su, holding tight on to the box, was just going to ask Winkie where at all he thought he was going, when the bank at the side dropped away. The surface changed, and—yes, they were out on a big road. "There," said Winkie triumphantly.

Su had just stubbed her toe. "I don't know what you mean by 'There'," she said crossly. "Where do you think we are anyway, Winkie?"

"Well," he said, "I just can't say right, but it's kind of like a main road, and maybe Lochgilphead or Tarbert at the end of it."

"All right," said Su, "which end?"

"Well, I suppose——" said Winkie, and hesitated. And then someone stepped out of the shadows and said, "A bonny nicht for the road, and a *been* young *rani*! Where is't you're going?"

"Oh," said Su, "will you help us? Who are you?"

"Ach, me is't? I'm guid-brither to wee 'Dina's old *mort*, and I ha' been about Port-na-Sgadan plenty. Are ye wanting back?"

"Yes," said Su, "oh yes!"

"Weel, maybe I shouldna be asking what ploys took ye to yon place at the back o' midnight. But ye're nane the waur. Excepting maybe ye could do wi' a bit *plasky*, Miss Susan?"

"I could," said Su, "and then to get home."

The man laughed, and gave a whistle. It was kind of nasty, the sound of yon hard whistle in the middle of the blackness, and for a moment there was a scare on both the two children. But they saw the black hump of a wattle, a tinker's tent, just off the side of the road, and a light stirring, and a dog growling but hushed, and then a woman's voice. She and the man talked quickly, and half in the tinker's speech with words of *plaskies* and *strods* and *tugs*. And Su kept whispering to Winkie, who was sore put about with it all, and kept fingering at the dirk, that it was all right. Here were folk that meant awful well by them, and so it turned out, for they brought a coat for Winkie, and an old brown plaid for Su. There were shoes, too, but they were nothing great, and no kind of fit, and the two felt they would do as well barefoot. Then the woman brought out two great pieces, cheese and smoke-tasting cold bacon between the thick bread. The two sunk their teeth in them. While they were at it, there was the noise of a lorry coming, and the headlights up the road. "Wait, you!" said the man, and stepped forward and held his hand up. For a time he was speaking to the driver of the lorry, then called over his shoulder, "Come your ways, now, come. *Bing* here! Ye'll be home soon enough."

They piled into the cabin of the lorry, and their friend stood back as the driver shoved the gear-lever home, and went rattling on, saying nothing, while Winkie and Su finished their pieces. At the turn south to Ardrishaig, he stopped to light a cigarette. He turned towards them, with the cupped flame lighting his face, and they were both puzzled, for they half knew him, and still and on they couldn't put a name on him. He said, "You know me, surely?"

At last Winkie said, hesitating, because it seemed a daft thing to say now. "Were you my enemy?"

"I was your prisoner," said the man, "and the swan-maid saved me."

"But who in all the world", said Winkie, "are you—now?"

"It is the queerest thing," said the lorry driver, "but I had no mind o' then till I saw you in my headlights, and maybe when you are away I will forget it again. Aye, aye, you have your dirk with you, *a charaid*. For we were friends afterwards."

"How were we?" said Winkie. "Was it after the judgment by the High Chief?"

"Aye, aye, and when you were a man grown."

"Oh," said Winkie, and gulped. "Yon years I should have had! What happened to me at all?"

The man got his cigarette well lit, and drove on between the tall dark houses of Ardrishaig, and past the harbour light, and the riding lights of the fishing boats. He was frowning, and spoke slowly. "As I mind on it," he said, "there was a change that came on you, and there were those who said the swan-maid was of God. That her doings over myself were the first miracle and marvel. Aye, the first of many. Yon one with the healing of the man born blind. And more that came with every telling of a tale that was told often enough. Aye, often enough, until such times as folk were not listening to such stories. Were told that they mustna listen. But only, maybe, to sermons." His voice seemed to have gone far off. You could hardly hear it above the noise of the engine. "But it was a great story for all that. Aye, aye."

"What story?" asked Winkie, bothered and impatient, for the man was speaking slower and slower, and at last had stopped speaking.

"Your own story," said the man. "The story of the saint. Did you not know? It was a saint's life you had."

"What, me?" said Winkie.

"Aye, you. Or the one whose shape you had taken and whose mind had been touched with other kinds of thoughts through your coming. For indeed it is a hard life, the life of a saint. And many a thing you wanted to do. Aye, you wanted it wild, but you didna do it for all that. Since there was this other thing. That began with the coming of the swan-maid, and the vengeance that you wanted to take, but you didna take." He said nothing for a time, but drove steadily along the road with the moonlight on the mackerel-scaled water beside it. Winkie felt kind of awkward speaking. It was beyond all queer to think of himself a saint. Not wanting to be but someway having to be. Having it laid on him the same as a blood feud, and as heavy. He sat nursing his dirk, and felt that Su was watching him, and not knowing what to say either. Because, if she herself was part of a miracle—well, that would be queer. Aye, queer altogether, beyond all telling.

They were half asleep now, sliding and jolted together on the torn leather of the lorry seat. The road slid back, mile after mile, under the lorry's wheels. And suddenly it was slowing, then it braked and stopped. They blinked and looked out into the black night that seemed to be greying a little in one corner. "I have gone a bittie out of my road to take you to Port-na-Sgadan," said the driver, "but I would want to repay you some way." He leaned over and shoved open the door of the lorry's cabin. "Yonder's the Tigh Mór."

"But——" said Winkie, stumbling out, and Su half tripped over her plaid, but landed on her feet, clutching on to the box. And the door slammed shut, and the lorry was away past them, its tail-lamp dimming along the road.

After a time Winkie said, "I wouldna like to be a saint —much." He shook his head uncomfortably. But Su was feeling a thing in her box, like the chipping of an egg. "Oh, do come on, Winkie!" she said, and started off up the avenue, walking on the grass at the edge. The moon had slid down to its setting now, but the pale beginnings of morning were getting clearer. The dark block of the Big House stood in front of them. No lights in the windows. No sounds.

Inside the box the thing was knocking and knocking. Winkie felt it, too. "What will we do?" he whispered.

"I think we ought to open it," Su said. "There's the nursery window." She pointed up to the big gable. Winkie nodded. They took the lid off cannily, meaning to look, but the golden nut flew past and it was whirled up like a comet, a spark of light, and disappeared through the window. They watched, holding on to one another.

And in a moment something else came out of the window, a blotch of darkness that spurted up against the stars above the gable, and then shot down towards them. As they ducked it tore round them, and Winkie gave a stab with the dirk, and in a moment the thing was hurtling back over the trees in the direction of the glen and Knocnashee. "Well!" said Winkie. Already the night was growing and the first colour creeping back into things. He lifted his dirk, and what was dripping from it was once again the green blood of yon other folk. He put out his finger and touched it, then made a face and wiped his finger quickly on the back of his shorts.

"Will it be all right now, Winkie?" asked Su. "Are you sure?"

"Aye, aye," said Winkie, "isn't it bound to be right now!" But some way he didn't seem as sure as when he was the Chief.

"I must see!" she said. "Come on in!" She took his hand and went quick through the cold dawn-wet grass to the side door past the wood-shed that was never locked. The stars were getting paler in the sky and then going out, and here and there in the bushes a bird beginning on the day. But he began to pull back. "Ach no, Su!" he said. "I dinna like!"

She stopped. "Why on earth not, Winkie?"

"Not to the Big House, Su! You've all your friends there. And me——"

"Nobody else did what you did for me," said Su, "so don't go and be silly just because it's now." And she gave him a tug that brought him in over the threshold. It was still night inside the house with the curtains drawn, and very quiet. They went up the stairs, hardly breathing, and along the passage. To-morrow she might look to see if there was a mouse-hole in the wainscot, but not now, not yet. She put her hand on the cool door-knob of the wee room and turned it and pushed softly, and still Winkie was holding her other hand. The curtain was pulled back and the room light enough for her to see. She went to the cot and knelt down beside it, peering through the bars. Donald was asleep with one hand up over his head clutching the leg of his woolly lamb. He was breathing very gently. "Donald," she whispered. "Donald, swee-tie——" And he opened his eyes and grinned all over and his hand uncurled from the lamb and reached through the bars and took a warm and loving grip of her nose. She found herself shaking all over. "Oh I was so frightened!" she said. "So awfully frightened. But it's all right. It's him."

"Nothing surer," said Winkie. "Didn't I tell you, Su. And now you should get to your bed before folks is about. And me the same."

"I'll see you down," said Su. She kissed Donald through the bars of the cot and tiptoed back and down the stairs to the door.

"Well——" he said, and then, "I'll need to be gone, Su."

"When will you be back, Winkie?" she said. "No, tell me! I've got to show you the guinea pigs yet."

"Ach, I don't know," he said and looked away and kicked at the turf.

"Please come," she said.

"Do you want me to come, truly, Su?"

"Yes," she said.

Still he stood swithering, and now it was full light and the sun would be on them in a moment. Suddenly he took Su's hand and shoved up the sleeve of the pyjama jacket. "Aye," he said, "the scar's on you yet, but not so bad, Su, not red. Just a wee white mark. But what in all the world will you say about it?"

Su looked at it. "But——" she said. "I've always had that mark! You know, it's a birth mark. Something you start with."

"You may have started with it, Su," he said, "but I made it with my arrow." He shook his head. "I will be around, Su, and I have my dirk yet, and maybe I will get the rest back the way the Brounie said. That could be, Su, couldn't it?"

"Of course," she said, "if you go on wanting it, the way he told you. And you will, won't you? But you'd better be getting back, Winkie, if you're going to get in without anyone seeing you. And you've got to come over in the afternoon. Say yes, Winkie! Say yes."

"Yes, Su," he said, and ran.